APOCALYPSE THE BLOSSOMING

THE POWER OF TWELVE BOOK TWO

MIRANDA MARTIN

CONTENTS

Foreword   vii

Chapter 1   1
Chapter 2   10
Chapter 3   13
Chapter 4   24
Chapter 5   26
Chapter 6   31
Chapter 7   37
Chapter 8   49
Chapter 9   66
Chapter 10   70
Chapter 11   78
Chapter 12   89
Chapter 13   96
Chapter 14   104
Chapter 15   118
Chapter 16   128
Chapter 17   135
Chapter 18   141
Chapter 19   155
Chapter 20   162
Chapter 21   169
Chapter 22   174
Chapter 23   177
Chapter 24   179
Chapter 25   184
Chapter 26   187
Chapter 27   190
Chapter 28   195
Chapter 29   204
Chapter 30   214
Chapter 31   223

Chapter 32   225

About the Author   233
Also by Miranda Martin   235

Apocalypse the Blossoming © 2019-2020 Miranda Martin

Originally published as Divine Magic (Fallen Revelations Book Two).

FOREWORD

Don't miss the start of *The Power of Twelve* start at the beginning if you missed it!

Apocalypse: The Beginning
By Miranda Martin

CHAPTER ONE

I startle awake, the remnants of another nightmare clinging to me. Sweat cools on my skin as I try to orient myself. A smooth stone wall that I don't recognize is next to me.

Breathe, Aviella. Stay calm.

Slowly, as the dregs of my nightmare pass, awareness returns. Someone's next to me. It's Efram. His chest rises and falls steadily. My heart slows, returning to a normal rhythm as I remember where I am—Bunker 2. Except it's not just Bunker 2. I'm in the underground of the underground Bunker 2. Try saying that one three times fast.

Efram stirs next to me. I'm glad I didn't wake him up, because he needs the rest. We've been waiting for days. The rebels are nice. Friendly. They're putting themselves at great risk hiding us, but we're still stuck. We need transportation out of here, and that's not easy. Unfortunately, I've become quite skilled at calling attention to myself. Thanks to my latest exploits, the Dragons who run Bunker 2 are not only aware of my powers, they want me. I can't imagine it's for good things.

It doesn't matter how much my father prepared me for the role I'm playing in the Apocalypse. I'm not ready. Without the support of my protectors, I have no doubt—I wouldn't have made it this far. Efram stirs next to me, rolling towards me, but he's still asleep. I study the Necroseer. His ink-black hair has fallen over his face, and it's perhaps the first time he's ever looked at peace with sleep hiding the sad, silver-violet of his eyes. He's kind and intelligent and dedicated. Everything a girl could want in a man. I can't help my smile or the urge to reach out and touch the several days' worth of beard growth on his jaw.

Before I can, I sense an energy nearby, and it pulls my attention away. I rise on one elbow and look over Efram's shoulder. Rafe is in the doorway.

Rafe is a demon, not that you'd know it by looking at him, unless you consider that he's devilishly handsome. Then yeah, Rafe definitely falls into that category. Heat flushes my cheeks at the sight of his open jacket, shirtless beneath, with intricate tattoos running the length of his sculpted chest up his neck. The tattoos are even on the backs of his hands. Rafe grins and takes a bite out of an apple. The loud, crisp crunch implies so many things to my imagination. His golden eyes promise delights out of this world. I've been resisting the desire since we've met, no matter how badly my body wants him. Rafe knows it, and being who and what he is, he takes great delight in toying with it.

He nods and motions at me with the apple then walks out of sight. Carefully I slide out the end of the bed, doing my best not to wake Efram. Outside the door, I look around but don't spot Rafe. I close my eyes and extend my senses. It's not something I completely understand, and I'm not even sure I can do it, but it seems like it might work. As my awareness expands, I sense traces of his energy, so I follow them and find him leaning against a column.

"You two are getting chummy," Rafe says, one eyebrow arching.

"Jealous?" I ask, returning the demon's own grin.

"We all belong to you, Aviella. You'll do with us what you choose," he says. He's a charming joker but there's an odd seriousness to his words.

I don't know what to say. Who am I to have collected these men who are so loyal to me? What did I ever do to deserve this? Rafe smiles as the silence between us stretches. He shrugs and starts walking, so I fall into step beside him. He leads the way through a series of small tunnels that wind between some old storage containers the rebels have spruced up to use as rooms.

It's the first time in a long time I've felt comfortable, but I know it's going to fade soon enough. I can feel it in my bones. I feel a lot of things. My gifts are becoming more sensitive. It's scary. All my life these gifts have been something to fear, to hide, things that set me apart from everyone else. They kept me alone, made me an outcast. Now that I'm with others who are also special, and I'm no longer alone, I'm having to come to terms with them. Before, I considered them bad, now I'm being shown that they can be used for good. That I can make a difference in the world. It feels right. Perhaps all my life and all the hardships were meant to lead to this.

Perhaps, or perhaps I'm just lucky. Lucky to have survived, lucky to have found friends like this, just… lucky.

As we pass by several of the empty rooms, the sound of soft conversation drifts down the tunnel, growing louder as we approach. Rafe leads the way into a converted container. Makeshift couches line the walls, and in the center of the space are several tables with chairs around them, most of which are occupied. At least a dozen people are hanging out. They look up as we enter with friendly smiles and a welcoming energy.

One older gentleman, probably in his late fifties, with silver hair and sharp blue eyes rises to his feet. Three other men sit at the table with him holding playing cards.

"Welcome," the man says. "I'm Peter. Would you care to join us?"

This is probably one of the biggest differences in this rebel underground from every other place I've been. They welcome people. They don't look at you suspiciously or appraise you for what they can get from you.

"What are you playing?" Rafe asks.

"Five card stud," the man replies.

"Well that's my game," the demon purrs, taking a seat at the table.

All of them look at me, so I shrug and take a seat too. I'm not sure about the rules of the game but I figure I can pick them up as I go. Peter sits down and takes up the cards. He does several fancy hand-to-hand shuffles, making it clear he's got skills. He deals us all in, and I watch.

"Would you like some wine?" Peter asks as he deals out the cards.

Rafe looks at me, his eyes dancing with delight. The smile that spreads across his face goes from ear to ear. I kick him under the table, but he barely winces. Jerk. There's no need to remind me of how I started this entire mess. I glare at him, willing him not to bring up the fact that I'm able to make my own wine.

"I'll pass, thank you."

"I'd love some wine," Rafe says, his eyes locked on mine. "How very friendly of you. Most places where we've been, people are not so open and sharing."

"We're rebels for a reason," Peter says. "We want to make the world a better place. Sharing wine is a starting point."

"An admirable goal," Rafe acknowledges.

We play through several hands, all of which I lose. It's fine with me not to win, but I am figuring out the rules of the game. We're on our sixth hand and it's down to Peter, Rafe, and me. The pot in the middle has grown quite large. We stare at each other with blank faces while I do my best to ignore what my senses are telling me. It's almost impossible. I know the other two are bluffing, I feel it.

Oh, what the hell.

"I'll see your bet," I say tossing another chip into the pile. "And I'll raise you, three more chores."

Money isn't any good here in the underground rebel society, so they trade chore time. It's sensible in a good way and makes the game have more value by putting something at stake. Peter squints, the slightest tightening of his eyes, but it tells me everything I need to know. He sighs then lays his cards down.

"Too rich for my blood," he says.

Rafe and I square off. I know he can sense me as well as I can sense him. It brings us to an impasse, and I'm not sure which one of us is going to be able to out-bluff the other one. He runs his fingers along his cards keeping his face unreadable.

"What's it going to be?" I ask.

"Well, little bird," Rafe says. He looks his cards over again and then smiles broader. "I'll see you."

He throws his chips into the center. He lays the cards out on the table with a flourish that only he could manage. There's an elegance to it, as well as a level of cheesiness that Rafe somehow manages to make sexy. I look over his hand and can't contain my smile.

As I lay my cards out, Rafe's face collapses because he sees that I've won.

"You're becoming quite good at this," Rafe says.

"I'll take that as a compliment," I say, pulling the chips towards me.

The sound of coughing underlies our conversation. It's loud and sounds painful. It's been going in the background through the entire game. I've done my best to ignore it, but something about it makes my heart ache. Rising to my feet I go to find its source.

"You're not gonna give us a chance to win anything back?" Peter asks.

"You all can keep your chores," I say. "I was only playing for fun."

A round of soft cheers from the players, then the coughing fit sounds again. I turn to follow the noise. Rafe takes his leave, and then he's beside me. Something about the sound sends a hand deep inside me where it grabs hold and pulls me along. I have to do something, anything to help.

The sound grows louder. It's high-pitched, pitiful, and obviously coming from a child. I walk through the opening of one of the storage containers, and Nathaniel is there. The warm-skinned angel turns as I enter and looks at me with dark, grim eyes. The sound is coming from behind him and I push past him to the source.

A little girl lies on a cot, hair stuck to her face with sweat. She's flushed. Tears are running down her face. She looks at me with feverish eyes, shivering. A pale woman sits beside her, wiping a damp cloth across her face. She starts coughing again, doubling over in pain as she does. Strangely, my hands grow warm. The coughing fit passes, and the girl looks at the woman.

"Mommy," she gasps.

"I know, honey, I know," her mother says, desperation in her voice.

"We're here, baby," a man says from the end of the bed.

I've seen him before. He's one of the leaders of the Rebels.

He looks over at me, shaking his head, jaw tight. Another woman emerges from a small side room, carrying a bowl of something. She stops when she sees me.

"You shouldn't be here," she says, shaking her head.

"I have to be," I say.

Strange words. I'm not sure why I said them, but I know they're true. This is where I need to be, right here, right now. The woman's eyes widen, her mouth tightens, then opens to argue.

"Nora," the man says. Tor, his name comes back to me. "Let her be."

Nora glances at him, frowning, then shrugs. My hands feel like they're on fire. I flex my fingers and look down at them. A soft glow is coming from them. The little girl looks past her mother at me. Her eyes pull me forward, and I kneel next to her. Moving on an instinct I don't understand, I place one hand on her forehead and the other on her stomach. A golden, glowing energy pours out, covering her small body.

She shudders and closes her eyes, and then color returns to her face. As my power grabs hold of me, it pours out and into the girl. It's draining me. I can't stop it. Throwing my head back I try to pull away, to stop it, but I can't. The edges of my vision turn gray and the room spins. The golden glow brightens until it's blinding.

Hands grab me by my shoulders and pull me back, breaking the connection. Waves of faintness pass over me, and I'm sure I'm going to pass out. My knees buckle, but Nathaniel catches me before I hit the ground.

"That's quite enough," the angel says.

His hands are warm where they touch me, flowing energy into me and restoring my reserves.

"Are you okay?" Rafe asks, concern in his voice.

"She'll be fine," Nathaniel snaps.

"Boys," I say. I want to say more, to stop them fighting but I'm so freaking tired.

"Mommy?" the little girl says, sitting up in bed.

I look at her and smile. Color has returned to her face, and it's obvious she feels better. I look at my hands with a sense of wonder. I had no idea I could do something like that. My gift is more multifaceted than I ever imagined. I can heal people? Maybe I can make a difference in the world. There are so many sick people. If I can bring them relief... this really would be a gift.

The man, Tor, walks over, his eyes glistening with unshed tears.

"Thank you," he says. "I'm indebted to you. I'll bring you to the crossing point of Wormwood myself when the sweeps die down."

"Do you have any idea when that will be?" Rafe asks.

"No," Tor says, frowning. "We're still hearing patrols overhead as often as not."

Nathaniel looks at Rafe and then at me. The three of us frown, wanting to hurry up and get out of here. Every day we're here increases our risk of discovery. It probably would've been a lot easier, okay scratch the probably, if I hadn't attracted the attention of the Dragons. I'll have to own that one. Bad Aviella.

Except I don't know how else I could've saved Nathaniel and Rafe, so I'm not going to apologize for it. Well any more than I already have. One way or another we have to get out of here. Every moment we're here it's not only us in danger but everyone around us. It doesn't help that I can feel myself being pulled forward. It's a calling that tugs at my soul. I'm not where I'm supposed to be.

Sighing, I shake my head and accept the gratitude and offer of help for what it is. It's all we have for now. The rebels are doing everything they can.

"Thank you," I say. "We do appreciate everything you have done for us."

"What you've done here won't be forgotten," Tor says.

I smile, place a hand on his arm, and squeeze.

Having done everything I can, I turn and leave. Trying to find something positive to focus on, I think about my newfound ability to heal. If I can help people like that, then maybe my existence in this desolate world that my generation has inherited really will mean something.

CHAPTER TWO

RAFE

I shouldn't be jealous but I am. It's more than being competitive with the angel, that's natural and expected. It's the way Nathaniel acts. The angel likes to lord it around like somehow I single-handedly ruined his life.

You'd think with the end of the world and all, he would get over the fact that his adopted father was a human with the same frailties as anyone else. So what if he had a title he didn't live up to. What parent does, when you think about it?

The angel could be thankful that he had a parent at all. A lot of us, including me, had to scrape by to survive. When you do that, you learn to appreciate the connections you do have with less judgment.

I've had my fill of his high and mighty attitude. The way he looks at Aviella makes my blood boil. Okay, I'll admit it, I am jealous and that's okay.

It's my turn to cook, so I go to the make-shift kitchen. As luck would have it, Nathaniel is leaning against the doorway. I wonder if he's waiting for me. He doesn't move as I approach, largely because he's an ass. I turn sideways and press past him.

I dig around for ingredients for something to make. Nathaniel continues glaring, but I pointedly ignore him. There's no reason to get into it. The only thing that would accomplish is upsetting Aviella.

"You can't be serious," Nathaniel says, at last.

Tensing, I suppress my furious reaction. I turn towards the angel slowly, still struggling to keep control of my temper.

"What is up your ass?" I growl.

Nathaniel stares at my pocket. The edge of the Crossing Key is just barely hanging out. Dammit. I didn't want him to know I had that.

"You have a Crossing Key! You could've used it when the Bunker was imploding," he accuses.

"It's not that simple," I reply.

"Bullshit. What if things had gone to hell!"

"Then I would've used it. It's got two uses. It's not something you waste on a simple deadie attack."

"It was a lot more than a simple deadie attack," Nathaniel argues.

"No, it wasn't, and you damn well know it," I reply.

"You know as well as I do that there were bigger powers behind that than a simple undead mob or locust swarm," he counters.

"If we're talking about what I 'know' then tell me, what are you hiding about Bunker 4?" I say, attacking. "I know you know more than you're saying."

It creates the effect I want. Nathaniel's face flushes red with anger. He starts to speak but only a sputter comes out.

"Yeah, exactly," I say, pressing my advantage. "Let's talk about who's being honest and who's not."

Efram appears behind Nathaniel. "Keep it down," he hisses. "She's going to hear you."

"Dammit," I curse. "See what you've done now."

Efram looks between Nathaniel and me, then shakes his head. "I don't know what's going on between the two of you, but it needs to stop—now. Aviella's under enough stress. We're her protectors. That has to override all other concerns."

Nathaniel regains his composure. His face is back to its normal, stoic, hard look. He nods sharply to Efram, glares at me, and then spins on his heel and walks away.

"What in the hell was that?" Efram asks me.

"Oh, you know," I say, giving my best smile. "Just a little friendly rivalry."

Efram shakes his head and walks out of the kitchen. An emptiness forms in the pit of my stomach. I shouldn't have lost my temper. Damn that angel. I can't let him get under my skin. Slamming cans and pots, I take out my frustration on the food I'm preparing.

CHAPTER THREE

"**W**ould you like more?" Rafe asks.

I can't hide my surprise. "Are you serious?"

"Yeah, there's plenty to go around," Rafe says, smiling.

"This is incredible," I say.

Rafe grabs my tray and goes back through the food line. I take the opportunity to look around the dining hall. Nathaniel walks in, and we lock eyes across the room. The now-familiar tightness in my core happens as soon as we see each other. He looks like he's about to walk my way when Rafe returns to the table. Nathaniel frowns, the smallest break in his façade, and turns away.

Rafe sets the tray down in front of me and returns to his seat across the table. I devour my second helping. The food itself is nothing outstanding, but the quantity of it! It's standard fare for Bunker life, Nutrimeal and simple grains that are grown hydroponically underground, but I've never seen it in such abundance. In the orphanage, "seconds" wasn't a word anybody knew.

I'm halfway through my second tray, with Rafe grinning

at me the entire time, when I decide to confront him. Nathaniel told me about the Crossing Key that Rafe has. The angel says Rafe could use that to open a portal we can travel through. His argument is it would've gotten us out of the dangerous situation we were in when Bunker E247 fell.

"So, about the Crossing Key —" I say, letting it hang between us.

Guilt is an adorable look on Rafe. His eyes widen and his grin falters.

"I'm saving it for an emergency," Rafe says.

"Uh-huh," I say, encouraging him to continue.

"Look," he says, "it's only got two uses. It's not something we want to pull out early."

I let him dangle on the hook for a while longer as he tries to explain. Mostly I'm giving him a hard time because I do understand. I can't help that I like watching him squirm.

"So, being surrounded by undead, the Admin, and his shadow masters, that wasn't time for the big guns?" I ask.

"Aviella, I'm afraid it could get much worse," Rafe answers, unusually serious for him.

"Or when I was being drained by the Dementor-thing on the train," I continue.

"We had that under control," Rafe responds, desperation in his face and voice.

"Yeah?" I ask, enjoying the teasing.

"You're teasing me," he says, a statement not a question.

"I would never," I say, unable to suppress my grin.

"My goodness, girl, you could become an excellent demon," he says.

"It's okay," I say. "I was just having fun with you. I think Nathaniel's being a bit overprotective. He's probably trying to compensate for whatever it is he's keeping from me that he knows about my dad."

"He'll spill it eventually," Rafe says, with utter confidence.

"What makes you think that?"

"He wouldn't be concealing if it weren't significant. Angels, unlike demons, are susceptible to guilt. He'll cave, I promise."

I laugh. It's hilarious that Rafe feels he can make such a promise, but I'll take it. Nathaniel keeps himself walled off. I only get glimpses of what he hides behind the walls, usually when we're alone.

In a lot of ways, Efram does the same thing, walling himself off, holding himself back around me. I've been doing my best not to think about what Nathaniel is hiding, because I need a level head, especially right now. I have to focus on what's happening here and making sure that I don't pull more undue attention down on myself. Not thinking about my dad makes that easier.

Not far away, Nathaniel rises from his table and takes his tray up to the stack where the rebels will clean it. There's a small window in the wall that the tray passes through, and people take it. Interestingly enough, they use fire to disinfect the metal trays, because even here in this apparent land of plenty, there's still a water shortage. After the Wormwood incident, not to mention the multiple nuclear devices that were detonated by the governments in an attempt to control the Apocalypse, water is one of the most precious resources left on the planet.

I try to catch Nathaniel's eye as he walks past our table, but he avoids my gaze. He probably thinks we're talking about him—which is true. We were. A pang of guilt stabs into my heart. I don't want to hurt him. It's really hard trying to balance the emotional needs of so many men.

I'll have to talk to him later. If only he and Rafe could get along better. It would make my life much easier. I suppose it's probably easier to expect the Apocalypse to end itself. There are better odds of it actually happening.

"He'll be fine," Rafe says. "Trust me, I know about these things."

"Because you're an expert in angels?"

"Because I'm all-around awesome," he grins.

Laughing, I stand up and take my tray. "You're impossible."

"Impossibly handsome? Impossibly intelligent? Impossibly clever?" he asks. "Yes, all of those would apply to me."

I can't help but laugh. It's hard to be serious with Rafe, but beyond his façade I know he really is intelligent, thoughtful, and one of my protectors. He'll do anything for me. Unfortunately, I also know, deep in my bones, he's going to have to. All the danger we've been through is nothing compared to what we have yet to face. I only hope we all make it.

"There you go," I say, pulling the covers up tight around Dorna's chin.

"Thank you," she says, smiling so big I can see her missing two front teeth.

I muss her hair, then rise. She has a small space of her own in her parents' bunk. Makeshift walls built out of crates separate it from the main space. Her mom looks up from the cup she was staring into when I come around the false wall.

"Tea?" her mom, Nina, asks.

"That'd be nice," I agree, taking a seat at the table.

She goes over to the counter and prepares a steaming cup of tea which she sets down in front of me. It has the slight scent of licorice. I sip it, carefully watching Nina.

"I want to thank you again," Nina says. "I don't want to think about what would've happened if you hadn't helped us."

"I'm just glad I could," I say.

"I don't know what I would do without her," Nina says, her eyes heavy and wet.

The worry has taken its toll. Crow's feet at the corners of her eyes and a perpetual frown make her look older than I think she is. Life in the Apocalypse isn't easy, but I'm sure it's even harder when you have a kid to worry about.

"She's going to be fine," I tell her, placing a hand on top of hers.

My hand grows warm, and I push a small trickle of my energy into her, intending to reassure, hoping it works. It's not something I'm sure I can do, but it feels right.

So much of what I've learned about using my powers has been through instinct or trial and error. I'm rewarded this time by seeing the tension drain out of Nina's face. She takes a deep breath and lets it out in a heavy sigh.

"You're an angel," she says, smiling for the first time since I've met her.

"I don't know about all that," I smile back. "Nathaniel's the angel. I just do what I can."

"Angels," Nina snorts. "They don't help anyone, not the way we were supposed to believe they would. You, you actually help."

"Thank you," I say, unable to meet the intensity of her stare.

She has no idea how much I'm winging this. I'm trying to do what I can as I'm pulled along a dark path that I never would've asked for. I guess I can thank my father for that.

The familiar, empty ache in my chest blossoms the moment I think of him. I miss him so much. I still know, or at least I feel, that he's alive. Out there somewhere, probably searching for me. He has to be, because I don't think I could face the world without knowing he's in it.

All my life he prepared me. Telling me I was special, how special my mom was, though I never knew her. I have a vague image of a face that I associate as having been my mom. When I think of her I feel warm, like I'm being embraced in love. I don't doubt she loved me, but dad never was clear on why she left or what happened. I always figured there was time to find out later. How wrong I was.

"All right," I say, finishing my tea. "I should let you get some rest too."

Nina smiles and nods. She walks with me to the door to their bunk. When we reach it, she grabs me awkwardly and pulls me into an embrace. I return it wholeheartedly. She's a good woman, trying her best to take care of her family. I admire her determination and strength.

Leaving Nina behind, I walk the mostly empty corridors. Restless energy making it clear sleep will elude me if I lie down. My thoughts circle back to my dad, no matter how hard I try to keep them from him. I'm being obsessive and I know it.

A fluttering sound catches my attention, pulling my thoughts away from the circling drain of depression. Wanting something, anything, to focus on outside myself, I decide to investigate. Following the fluttering noise, I look into an open bunk and there's Nathaniel.

The angel is shadow sparring with himself. It's something we've all been doing to keep ourselves sharp. My breath catches in my chest as I watch. There is grace and beauty in his motions. He's taken off his shirt and has revealed his wings, something I've rarely seen.

As he goes through the stances of his fighting motions, he uses his wings to his best advantage. Leaping into the air and hanging there, beautiful white wings slowly stroking to keep himself aloft. A soft silvery glow engulfs him.

Desire pounds through my veins. My cheeks warm, and my skin becomes feverish. An overwhelming urge to feel his skin against mine floods through me. It's ridiculous.

Nathaniel keeps himself distant. It's not that he doesn't want me—I can feel that in his energy—it's that he won't give into it.

I shouldn't give in either. What right do I have to claim even a moment like that with everything happening around us? It would be extraneous. Also, as much as I hate to admit it, how would I balance it with the other guys in my life? I'm not sure, still, how I went from being a complete and total social outcast to the center of attention for so many strong, handsome, sexy men. It makes me uncomfortable, but at the same time it makes me feel special.

Nathaniel is floating in the air about four feet off the floor when he turns and looks at me. I smile and wave, to which he silently nods. He looks serious, but that's normal for Nathaniel. He holds up one hand and motions with his fingers that I should come closer. It reminds me, for all the world, of that scene from *The Matrix* when Neo and Morpheus are going to fight. Great, this is not exactly what I had in mind.

While it may not have been exactly what I intended, there is a touch of romance to it. The slight upturn at the corner of his lips, the light in his eyes, but mostly the way his energy feels. Having nothing better to do and knowing that sleep will elude me anyway, I nod and approach. He doesn't wait. As soon as I step inside he attacks, diving towards me.

I slam my forearms together in front of me, pulling my magic with the motion. It forms a shield, and Nathaniel bounces off. He doesn't hit hard, which tells me he was ready for that maneuver. He glides to the ground, and his wings disappear.

In a way, that's a dirty trick. It's how the Angels hide among us, which they've done since the dawn of time. Only the sensitives throughout history ever knew of them, and of course everyone thought they were crazy or fanatics. Surprise! The Apocalypse has vindicated those poor souls.

"Well done," Nathaniel says.

"Thanks, Efram's shown me a few tricks."

He nods with the barest of grimaces. Ignoring his expression, I settle into fighting form. He does the same, and we move through different stances before working our way back up to sparring.

"Let me show you something," Nathaniel says.

He steps behind me and wraps his arms around my waist. My skin burns where his touches it. I imagine I feel his excitement too, but I'm not sure. He places one hand on my stomach as his other slides out along my left arm. He pushes on my hips so that I rock back and forth.

"You have to keep your hips loose," he says. "It makes you able to pivot, to adjust to the changing fight."

"But how do I get my power?" I ask.

"Your power comes from your ability to adapt," he answers.

"Efram says I have to plant my feet and pull strength from the earth. That planting my feet is the base from which my power flows."

"Yes, he's not wrong," Nathaniel says. "That only applies when you're actually punching, though. Before and after that you should be fluid and ready to move."

He continues working with me, but I'm finding it hard to concentrate with his body so close to mine. Fire burns where he touches me. I do my best to focus, pushing aside my more carnal thoughts because there really is no time for them.

We drill with his maneuver for what feels like entirely too long. It's not that I don't think it's a good maneuver, it's the distraction of him pressing against me. Is he doing it because he likes it too? No, not Nathaniel, right?

"Yes, exactly like that," he compliments me when I finally get it right.

"Yeah, I get it. It does feel better," I agree.

"There's another trick I'd like to show you," he says. "You can use the sigils I've put on you to create effects. The ones you have now will let you do something like this," he says.

He waves his hands in the air, and a mist forms in front of him. It's a thick fog which is hard to see through. He turns sideways, steps into it, and then suddenly disappears. Before I can turn a circle, he taps me on the shoulder.

"Hi," he says, and I jump in surprise.

"How did you do that?" I ask.

"The sigils I've put on you can manipulate light," he says. "Handy for when you need to duck out of the way."

"Show me!" I say, excitement bubbling in my stomach.

He places his hands on my arms, sliding the sleeves of my blouse up past my elbows to reveal the silvery sigils inscribed on my skin. Warmth flushes along my exposed skin trailing behind his touch. Soft, gentle, yet firm, he grips my wrists. Our eyes lock, and my mouth and throat go dry. My core tightens like a spring ready to explode. His lips part, soft air slipping past them. I lean in towards him, involuntarily.

"Move like this," he says, pulling my arms through circular motions.

My body follows his, but my eyes and heart follow his face. His strong jawline, eyes like deep pools, a day's shadow on his chin. His firm grip guiding, controlling, yet giving me control too. I step closer, rising on my toes, lips moving towards his. He pauses, staring down into my eyes, the magnetic attraction between us undeniable. He moves towards me, this is it, then he hesitates. His lip quivers with barely controlled desire.

Screw it, I'm doing this, I decide, rising to meet his lips.

A silver light engulfs me, and the room disappears in a flash....

～

I STUMBLE FORWARD, BARELY CATCHING MYSELF BEFORE I FALL. My head is spinning, and I'm completely disoriented.

"Nathaniel?" I ask, trying to focus my eyes.

"I'm here, Aviella," he replies.

I keep blinking until the silver light finally clears and I can see again at last—only now we are not alone.

"What in the hell?" I ask.

Killian stands behind Nathaniel, smiling. Gavin, Ronan, and Luca are beside him, all of them focused on me. My heart skips a beat and my cheeks flush hot. The magnetic pulse of attraction with the mages threatens to override my good sense.

"Hey, there," Gavin says. "Welcome back."

Their magic weaves its way into my energy. Ronan scans me which opens the pathways between us, and I sense he's straining to hold back the intensity of his attraction for me. It seems he's struggling particularly hard to control it, barely containing himself. My skin burns hotter, feeling his desire so hot and barely kept in check.

One thing is for sure, the connection I have with all of the mages is getting deeper. It must be supernatural in nature. It's overriding good sense and nature. Unbidden, an image flashes through my head of what would be like to be taken by all four of them.

Good Lord, I'm not that kind of girl, am I?

"Why are you guys here?" I ask, struggling to focus on anything that will help me control the volatile emotions and desires raging in my body.

"We go where we're needed," Gavin says.

"Well that's appropriately vague," I respond, crossing my arms over my chest.

Gavin's grin widens as if he's proud of himself. Jerk.

"He's been practicing," Luca quips.

Nathaniel grimaces, looking uncomfortable.

"Okay, so what happened?" I ask. "Nathaniel and I were sparring, and then everything went silver and white and I kind of saw some images…"

"What kind of images?" Gavin asks, suddenly serious.

He motions with one hand, and Luca and Ronan move to stand on either side of me.

"I'm not sure," I say, biting my lower lip.

Luca and Ronan hold their hands up, palms facing me then move them up and down about a foot away. Warmth floods through my skin as they move through my energy field and their magic touches me.

"Hold still, we need to check this out," Ronan says.

"I'm fine," I argue.

"Aviella, let them help," Nathaniel says.

I roll my eyes but hold still while they do their work.

CHAPTER FOUR

NATHANIEL

I watch as the mages fawn over her. It's almost more than I can stand. My blood runs hot, and my heart beats faster. Tension floods my muscles, and there's an overwhelming urge to hit one of them. I struggle with it and finally manage to get it under control.

What in the hell is wrong with me?

I'm jealous. This is wrong. I can't be falling for her. I can't but sparring with her was electric. The desire between us is a heavy gravity pulling me ever closer. It would be easier if only I wanted her, but I feel she wants me as well.

When I was close to her, holding her, helping her through the moves... I was barely able to hold onto my concentration.

Duty. I have my duty. I cling to that.

The mages are examining her aura, searching as they try to find the source of what happened. It was powerful, I saw when it took hold of her, and I have my suspicions about its source. Ronan moves his hand over her chest so close that I can see he brushes her breast. Anger, white hot and instant, flashes. I clench my jaw and my fists tighten. They'd best be careful. She's not dropping any hints, and they shouldn't get the wrong idea.

I can't get the feeling of her body pressing against mine out of my head. She is so perfect, one of God's greatest creations. I almost slipped, failing in my duty to protect her. Giving in to base desires.

It's a good thing that the mages showed up when they did. If she hadn't been taken by that vision, I would've failed. The raspberry flesh of her lips so close to mine. I wouldn't have been able to resist.

"I'm just fine," Aviella complains, not for the first time.

I look away. Looking at her with the mages surrounding her makes my chest ache. I should put some space between the two of us but first I must get her somewhere safe.

Listening to her argue with the mages, I contemplate possible outcomes. Silas insists that Tynan won't harm her, and I believe him. He's always been cautious. If he says something, you can count on his word. When we get to Bunker 3, I should take off. I've been ignoring my other duties for a while in favor of her. I know that the mages won't be far, and Efram and Silas will be with her as well.

And, as much as I hate to admit it, Rafe will be with her too. He's a formidable force in his own right. Despite being who and what he is.

I should be tracking down the other special wards. I can do that faster alone than traveling with a group. It would put me more on purpose with what I'm supposed to be doing. Yes, this is a plan.

"If you are quite finished, I think I'm ready to try to draw what I saw in the vision," Aviella says.

"I'll grab some paper," I say. "And Silas, he'll want to see this."

CHAPTER FIVE

*E*veryone watches as I sketch out the symbols the best I can. I'm no artist, but the shapes are there at least. As I finish the last one, my protectors lean in, jostling each other as they try to get a closer look. One by one they shake their heads, exchanging looks before they step back.

Standing in the circle of men, I feel the connection I have with each of them like a magnetic line between us. Pulsing, alive, and shifting with the passing moments. Each of them is attractive, in his own unique way, but it's not their looks that draws me in. I'm bound to each of them. It's undeniable, and if it would stop there, I'd have nothing to worry about, but it doesn't. My life couldn't be that simple, could it? Of course not. I'm me. Social outcast extraordinaire, who somehow ends up with a gaggle of men, all of whom fawn over me. They want me, and perhaps worse, I want them. Each of them or all of them.

It should be nice. Every girl's fantasy, right? Yeah, sure, except the fantasy doesn't include feelings or jealousy or worrying about what each of them thinks not only of me but each other. On one hand it doesn't matter. I've not done anything with any of them. Well, I've been close with Rafe.

As if he's reading my thoughts, the demon looks at me with a sparkle in his eye. Damn if that doesn't turn me on. I love his carefree attitude. His approach to everything is that we've got this, no matter how grim it is.

Silas, studious, intelligent Silas stares at the symbols the longest. All of us watch him. He's the librarian, the sexy librarian. That makes me giggle, and they look at me when it slips out. When they see me flushing with embarrassment, Rafe gives a slow grin and Gavin smirks.

I shrug, dodging the attention, my arms and cheeks burning hot. An image flashes fast through my thoughts of all of them surrounding me, like this, but with significantly less clothing on. My cheeks become an inferno.

Rafe slips closer, and once more I wonder if the demon is reading my thoughts. I tense as he places his hand on my lower back, a knowing look on his face. No, Rafe, no way. He can't be in my head, can he? Damn it, get it under control, Aviella.

"I don't know," Silas speaks at long last.

The tension in the room deflates like a balloon losing all its air in one fast blast. I realize then all of us were hanging our hopes on Silas knowing what the symbols are. Damn it.

"We can consult our texts," Killian offers.

"The symbols are ancient," Gavin says.

"Yes, I know. I sense that much too, but I can't place them," Silas says.

The look on his face says it all. Admitting defeat is hard for him. Knowledge is his area, not knowing something bothers him, a lot.

"What's a little mystery among friends?" Rafe jokes.

It does nothing to lighten the mood. Nathaniel and Efram

step away from the group whispering to one another. The tension they're feeling pulses in our connection.

"I have an idea of where to look," Ronan says, crossing his arms over his chest and looking grim.

I wait for him to elaborate, but he doesn't say anything further. Helpful, Ronan, real helpful.

"It doesn't matter if that's all you know, you need to tell them," Efram says loud enough to draw everyone's attention.

Nathaniel is tense, shoulders hunched, staring at the ground with his back to us. He shakes his head then slowly turns around and walks over to the table with the rough sketches I made. He touches one of them before meeting my eyes.

"They're tied to your blood," he says.

"I'd agree with that," Silas adds.

"Okay…" I say, trailing off to encourage him to continue.

Nathaniel, being him, doesn't say another word. Damn, that angel is frustrating as hell! I wonder if he shouldn't actually be a demon!

"What does that actually mean, Nathaniel?" I ask.

"I do not know," he says, shaking his head. "It's something I…know."

"Great, helpful," I say, angrily.

"Maybe it is," Killian says, jumping in. "It gives us another direction in which to research."

"See, everything is coming together just fine!" Rafe says, ever the optimist.

Nathaniel glares while everyone else ignores his enthusiasm. Personally, I find it infectious. It's one of the things about him that I find attractive. No matter how grim things look he finds a way to see the good in them. Weird, considering what he is, but I'll take it.

Silence falls across our group, all of us staring at the

strange symbols on the paper. Efram shakes his head at last throwing his hands up in frustration.

"It is what it is," he says. "It might be a clue, but it does nothing to change our situation. We have to get Aviella out of here, away from the Dragons. They're still looking for her above us, and the longer we hide down here, the more likely they are to figure out where she is. Once they have their hands on her, we'll never see her again."

"Right," Nathaniel agrees with him.

Silas looks away, deep in his own thoughts.

"Are we any closer to an out?" Rafe asks.

"Tor is going to open a Crossing Point," Silas says. "He's gathering the last of the necessary materials."

"A Crossing Point?" Killian asks, eyes widening. "That's big magic, how in the nine hells is he going to pull that off and not have the Dragons right up your backsides?"

"We have a plan," Silas says.

Something about the way he says it stops the conversation. Silas looks serious and willing to brook no one questioning him. Killian's mouth opens like he's going to argue but then snaps shut as he decides better of it.

"Okay, then," Rafe says, but even he seems subdued.

"Guys," I say. "It will be all right. I trust Tor. He's smart, and he's led the rebellion here for a long time, keeping his people safe and saving hundreds from the system above them. It'll be okay."

"Right," Rafe says. "Now how about those symbols?" He points at the papers.

"I'm not sure there are any books left on Earth that will define them for us," Nathaniel says.

"Yet you think they're tied to her blood?" Ronan asks.

"Yes, that I'm sure of," Nathaniel says. "They are ancient. Very, very ancient."

"Then we'll do what we can," Gavin says. "Until then, we carry on."

"Yay," I say. "Carry on like nothing's changed. Right."

"Cheer up, beautiful," Rafe says, placing an arm over my shoulders. "Look at all these fine specimens of manhood, all here to do your bidding. What more could a girl ask for?"

My cheeks become an inferno, as once more I'm left wondering if the demon is reading my thoughts, or I'm just that easy to read. I've got to get out of here, now.

"Yeah," I choke out, my throat too tight for more words.

I turn and head for the door without a word, wanting nothing more than to get out of this uncomfortable situation.

"Be careful," Nathaniel calls after me.

"Aren't I always?" I ask, swallowing hard to force down the lump in my throat.

CHAPTER SIX

"*How's* Dorna?" I ask Nora.

Nora looks weary, and there's a heaviness to her spirit. Dark circles under her eyes and the frown lines at the corners of her lips tell me a lot. She forces a smile, but it dies before fully forming.

"Better," she says.

"Yeah?" I probe.

Nora sighs, shoulder slumping and head bowing. She stares at the ground between us for a long moment before she speaks.

"Yes," she says at last. "She is better."

"Good?" I make it a question. The fact she's not telling me something is obvious.

Her shoulders shake then her whole body is trembling. Her hair hangs over, hiding her face. Seeing the woman like this, an ache throbs in my chest. I want to take her pain away. Warmth floods through my body as magic swells inside me. Instinctively, I place a hand on Nora's arm, and through that connection her exhaustion rushes at me. It's an overwhelming blackness, more than any person should ever have to face alone.

My hand faintly glows, magic pulsing as I push it out and into her. Nora looks up, eyes widening, mouth dropping open as the warmth of it pushes into her. A light ignites in her eyes as the weight on her eases. The corners of her lips twitch, then a smile forms. A full, real smile. The first I've seen from her.

"Wha-" she doesn't finish the word, shaking her head and sighing. "Thank you."

"It's nothing," I say, smiling.

On one hand it is, if for no other reason than I have no idea what I just did. It'd be great to actually know what I'm doing or feel like I'm in control. Efram and Silas always know exactly what they're doing, what to expect when they weave magic. No such luck for me. I'm as likely to turn water to wine as I am to blow up the room I'm standing in.

It's always been this way. Coming unbidden, feeding off my emotions and causing problems for me. The story of my life. Growing up I was so scared of my powers I called them *it*. The monster that came unbidden and created chaos around me. Now, understanding better what they are, I still think of them in mostly the same terms. They create as much chaos as they do good.

"Would you like something to eat?" Nora asks.

"Nah, I'm good," I say. "I would like to see Dorna if I can."

"Of course," she says. "Tor is with her in her room. Please, go on in."

Their home is small, of course, Bunkers have limited space, and an underground rebel base under the underground limits space even more. Tor looks over as soon as I enter the door, having heard my arrival.

"Hello," he says, one hand resting on his daughter who's lying in her bed.

"How is she?" I ask.

"Better," he says, speaking softly.

Dorna's chest rises and falls evenly and she snores lightly. A soft sheen of sweat covers her forehead but her color is so much better than when I saw her before so I'm sure she is getting better.

"Good," I say, walking over to stand next to him. "Mind if I sit with her a bit?"

He frowns looking from his daughter to me. He's going to say no, I think for a moment. Tor is like a bear with a cub, big and burly and not going to let anything happen.

"Yeah," he says, rising to his feet. "I'll get something to eat."

"Cool," I say, taking his place at her side.

Up close it's obvious how much better she is doing. She's still weak from the ravages of her illness but she's no longer knocking on death's door. Her eyes flutter open.

"How are you?" I ask.

"Better," she says, her voice is hoarse but getting stronger. A half-smile lifts the corners of her lips.

"Good," I reply.

"I had a dream last night," she says.

"Oh yeah?"

"Yeah," she says, her eyes dropping away from mine as she frowns.

"What was it about?"

"You," she responds.

"Me?" I ask, surprised. Maybe I shouldn't be, I did save her life. She nods but doesn't say anything. "So, what happened in your dream?"

"There was this... light. A tunnel thing and you were going through it..."

"Uh-huh," I say encouraging her to continue.

"You broke through time but when you did there was a

bad person waiting for you," she says. "It's evil. It's trying to catch you."

Cold chills run up and down my spine. Her words echo through my thoughts and the symbols I saw in my vision come to mind as well as the ones I've seen on the undead that I've fought already. Is there something behind all of this? A single force? My stomach sinks as I think about it. I'd assumed everything was just... I don't know. Random? Chaos and my own bad luck. Surely it can't be planned, can it? When are there too many coincidences for it to be a coincidence? What does she mean by breaking through time? Too many questions.

"Well it's a dream, nothing to worry about, right?" I say, trying to keep my concerns out of my voice.

"I don't think it was..."

"I know," I say, leaning close to her and whispering in her ear. "But you know what? I got this."

I muss her hair and smile. She looks up at me, eyes wide, and a slow smile forms on her face.

"Yeah," she says, nodding. "You do."

"Good, kiddo."

"I need to check her vitals," Nora says, startling both of us.

"Okay," I say. "I'll check in on you later, okay?"

"You promise?" she asks.

"You bet," I say.

"Okay, good."

My thoughts run in a circle as I leave their space. Something about her words ring deep inside. I feel truth in them. I'm so distracted I run into someone.

"Sorry-" I start looking up into Gavin's grinning face.

"No problem," he says, smiling from ear to ear. "I love it when a pretty girl wants to press up against me."

"I didn't-" I start, cheeks burning.

His energy envelops me, intertwining with mine and I swear it feels as intimate as if he was exploring my depths physically, somehow more intimate. My body responds to it as I would to the touch of a lover. Flushing hot, core tightening, desire clouding rational thought. My mouth is dry, and I can't form words out of the chaos of thoughts spinning around. If he's here, he can't be alone…

Yup, there they are. The other three mages are fanning out behind him, all of them looking at me. Their energies pulse against me, filling my head with crazy thoughts, wild, insane ideas of what it might be like to give myself to my most carnal desires. If all four of them were focused on my pleasure…

Aviella!

Mentally I force myself to focus. Stupid, crazy thoughts, why do they make me feel this way?

"What are you doing here?" I snap, anger helping me get control of my runaway mind.

He looks past my shoulder, so I follow his gaze and see Dorna.

"No," I breathe.

"Yeah," he says. "She's special. We need to move her for her own safety."

"You have no idea how bad an idea that is," I say.

"We don't have a choice, she's in danger here," he says.

Killian walks up next to us and places a hand on my shoulder. My knees turn to water, and it's an effort to keep myself standing. I want to melt into him at his touch.

Damn it, Aviella, get a grip!

Gavin touches my face, placing his finger just below my ear and tracing the line of my jaw. A trail of fire follows the passage of his finger. I'm breathing in short gasps, and my heart pounds in my chest. A whimper tries to escape my lips, but I bite it off before it can get out. I'm not giving in. Nope, not going to do it, no way in hell I'm doing this. I can't hide the shiver that runs down my spine though. Damn it. Gavin grins even wider.

"Tor is never going to hand her over to you," I say.

Focus, Aviella. Tor, Dorna, important things, anything beside the way their energy is weaving in and out of yours. No, not his eyes, don't look there, or crap, not those bulging arm muscles either. Desperate I focus on the ceiling above us and try to get myself under control. It helps, a little.

"He can't protect her," Killian says.

"He won't believe that," I say. "It's his daughter, you have to get to know him. Let him get to know you," I say, studiously keeping my eyes on the ceiling.

"What are you looking at?" Gavin asks, looking up himself.

"Nothing," I snap.

Luca laughs, loud and brash, and my cheeks burn.

Damn it, why can't all of you just be... ugly or something.

"Okay," Gavin says, playing along. "So... Dorna?"

"Get to know Tor," I say. "You have to earn his trust. Once you do that you'll have your in."

I see him look at the others by the turning of the top of his head, just inside my line of sight while I continue inspecting the ceiling.

"We'll do it," Gavin says.

"Good. I've got to go," I say, pushing my way past them before I drop my eyes down.

I feel their eyes on me as I walk away, but more than that, I feel their energy clinging to me like the last lingering touches of a lover. Stiffening my spine, I do my damnedest not to let my hips sway or give any other encouraging motions. Good God, this is my life. What in the hell is going to happen next?

reaking through time, I think. *What does she mean?*

It's late, and almost no one is out as I pace the tunnels of the rebel home. I can't sleep. I keep thinking about what Dorna said. An enemy is waiting. There is some strange truth to her words that resonates deep inside. I keep feeling like there's something I should remember, but I can't quite put my finger on it.

The symbols I saw in my vision, the marks on the undead, the way my magic is growing, it's all related. Somehow. If only I could figure it out. I don't know what I expect of myself on this. I have all these people trying to help me, and none of them are doing any better than I am, and they're all a lot smarter than I am.

It's frustrating. If my dad were here, he'd have an answer. He always had an answer. Of course he would probably say it was all part of the plan. He talked often about the 'plan,' but when he said it with such confidence, you couldn't help but believe him. Then he'd remind me how much my mom loves me. I don't doubt she did, but she's gone. Like he is.

In a lot of ways, I'm still alone. Despite all my protectors.

Okay, Aviella, that's enough of the darkness. Focus on what is at hand.

Those damn symbols. They mean something, but what? What did Dorna mean I broke through time? Is she referring to the Crossing Point? I've never seen one, but they are a magic portal, maybe that's what she's referring to. If she is, does that mean an enemy is waiting for me on the other side?

Of course there's going to be an enemy waiting. How else would my life go?

Someone walks past me, casting a sidelong glance as they do. It pulls me out of my introspective thoughts. Several other people are now walking the hallways, and I suddenly realize I've paced the halls all night long. Dammit, I really should've slept. My stomach grumbles, reminding me of the basic need to eat. I make my way towards the mess hall.

The early morning shift is just starting, so there's only a handful of people at the tables. No one pays any attention to me as I walk in and make my way to the serving line. I still can't get over the abundance of food here. I've only recently gotten to the point that I don't feel like my eyes are bigger than my stomach. I go to an empty table with my loaded plate, sit down, and begin eating. I'm halfway through my plate when Efram joins me.

"Good morning," he says.

His steely eyes bore into me as if looking for some answer, but to what I'm not sure. I meet his gaze, admiring the strong jaw, and his overall presence. Efram is steady and loyal and filled with honor. I'm so comfortable with him, at times I forget how good-looking he is. My stomach tightens as desire flashes white hot.

"Morning," I say, forcing a mouthful of food down past the lump in my throat.

"I'm not sure about this crossing," Efram says.

"Oh yeah?"

"I'm worried that it will attract the Dragons' attention," he says. "I don't see how we could possibly open a portal without their knowing it."

"Silas says he has a plan," I reply.

Efram frowns and his eyes narrow. He shakes his head negative.

"I know what he says," he answers.

"Do you have a better idea?" I ask.

"I think we could —"

Something changes. Efram stops mid-sentence. A silence falls across the room that makes the hair on my arms stand up. Everyone looks at each other. No one says a word. Distantly something thuds. One thud, another thud, then yet another. My stomach sinks, and bile rises in my throat. Boots. It's the sound of boots.

Efram and I exchange a glance, and then we're both running. As soon as we exit the Mess Hall into the main tunnel, Ronan and Luca come running at us. They don't bother with words, grabbing me by either arm and dragging me along with them.

Glancing over my shoulder, I make sure Efram is keeping up with us. I want to protest but I'm not stupid. I don't know if the Dragon guards are inside the Bunkers yet or if they're just coming, but making noise is not a good idea.

They're dragging me deeper into the underground. Away from the entrance, which is probably smart. We find our way through milling crowds of scared people.

We come to a blank wall. The mages tuck me into a small space between the blank wall and one of the shipping containers the rebels use as bunks. The mages stand side-by-side blocking the entrance and protecting me. It hits me we're missing Efram.

"Where's Efram?" I whisper, voice quivering.

Rowan looks over his shoulder and shakes his head,

shrugging. Luca glances around but then places a finger over his lips. The silence across the rebel underground is oppressive. No matter that I saw all those people, it's too quiet. The sound of boots echoes again. It's above us, but it's coming closer. Somehow, I know we've been found out. I try not to think about it. I don't want to know that this is all my fault too. No matter how I try to push that thought away, it keeps creeping in. Memories of Bunker E247 rise, unbidden and unwanted. All those people, lost, because of me.

Dammit, there has to be something I can do to change things. What's the point of having all this power if I can't help anybody?

Footsteps echo, coming closer. My skin tingles as magic rises, preparing to fight. The sigils that Nathaniel put on me glow, brightening the dimness around me. Ronan and Luca shift their stances, preparing for a fight as well.

Rafe and Nathaniel step around the corner and we all relax. I slip between Ronan and Luca to peer down the hall, hoping to see Efram. It's empty though. My skin crawls as the sound of the boots grows louder.

"Where is he?" I whisper.

"He'll be here," Rafe says.

Ronan and Luca grip my shoulders and push me back. I resist, irritated by their overprotectiveness. When they continue pushing, I whirl around, shoving an open hand against each of their chests.

"No," I whisper through clenched teeth.

They exchange a glance with each other, and Luca bites his lower lip while Ronan's grip tightens. I glare at them until they back down. When they take their hands off my shoulders I nod emphatically and turn back around to look for Efram. I reach out with my senses, hoping I can feel him. Nathaniel places a hand on my shoulder, and I jerk my head towards him, ready to admonish him as well. Something in his eyes stops me. He leans in close and whispers.

"Aviella, that is not a good idea," he says. "They can sense your use of magic."

I want to argue with him. Fire burns through my blood, a burning desire to tell him how wrong he is. Except he's not and I know it. I'm being foolish. This is the exact kind of thing that is always getting me into trouble. As much as I want to disagree, he's right, so I stop. It makes me sick to my stomach. Once more, I can't do anything effective. So I wait.

Minutes crawl by, sliding into each other. Each one feels like an hour. We don't speak, unwilling to risk the extra attention. Not for the first time, I realize patience is not my strong suit.

There's the sound of an explosion and we all jump. This is going south fast. I look at my friends, my protectors, and I make a decision. I can't stand by and let this happen. I burst into action. Leaping forward, I run.

"Aviella, no!" Nathaniel screams.

Chaos erupts, and it seems everyone loses their minds, forgetting the danger of the Dragons.

I don't look back. I have to help. I am not going to stand by and let another Bunker fall because of me. Once was enough. I don't care what the Dragons do to me if I can't face them down. I won't let them harm these innocent people in their quest for me.

I hear cursing from over my shoulder, and I glance backwards. It's a mistake, because the moment I do, I run into something hard. It makes my head spin and knocks me to the ground. I look around, confused. A moment before there was nothing there, and I still don't see what I ran into. There's nothing but empty space ahead of me.

Luca walks up with a half-smile on his face. He holds a hand out to me, and I accept it. He pulls me back to my feet.

"What the hell was that?" I ask. "What about magic pulling the Dragons down on us?"

"You can't do this, Aviella," Luca says. "And they're going to find us anyway. We have to get out of here, now more than ever."

"I know how bad you want to help," Rafe says. "I get it, believe me. We all do. You have to realize, you're more important."

"No!" I yell. "It's not right and it's not fair. I'm no more special than any of these people. They have every much as right to live as I do."

"The Dragons won't harm them. They want you. The only way you can save these people is to escape. You have to. It's your destiny," Nathaniel says, his anger pounding against me.

I've never felt the angel's anger before. It's white-hot and burning and filled with a righteousness that melts my resolve to stand against him. Tears fall down my face. Frustration, anger, and more, because I know he's right. No matter how much I don't want it to be, I can't change the truth.

Tears well up in my eyes. I do my best to fight them, but there's no holding them back. I wipe at my cheeks furiously.

"Dammit!" I yell, shaking my fist in the air.

The men exchange a glance, and then Rafe steps forward and wraps his arms around me.

"Shhh," he says, running his hands through my hair.

"It's not fair," I say, tears flowing freely. "It's all my fault."

"It's not," Rafe says. "It's this world. Everything has led to this, since long before you were even born. Mankind has made his choices, and this is the world he's created. It didn't have to be this way."

"What's happening?" Efram asks.

I push away from Rafe but let a hand linger on his chest to show him I am grateful for his support. I wipe my eyes on my sleeve before looking at Efram. Tor and Dorna are with him. Dorna's eyes widen when she looks at me, and then she runs across the distance between us and leaps into my arms. She squeezes me tight and plants a big kiss on my cheek.

"It will be all right," she says, and her voice is sweet.

"Of course it will," I say, encouraging her optimism.

What else can I do?

Gavin and Killian stand behind Tor. We're all here except Silas. I don't want to leave without him.

"I can't open the crossing here," Tor says. "It's too close to the Dragons. They'd be on us in an instant."

"Do you have a better idea," Gavin asks.

"Yeah," Tor replies. "Follow me."

"We can't go yet," I say. "Silas isn't here."

"He can take care of himself," Efram says.

"That may be true," I reply. "It doesn't change the fact that he should be with us. He has no way of knowing where we're going."

"Aviella, we don't have time for this," Rafe says.

"What if it were you?" I ask, arching an eyebrow at the demon. "You'd want me to just leave you behind?"

"It's not —" Rafe says.

"It is exactly," I say, cutting him off.

I glare at each of the men, forcing them to bow to my will. I'm not leaving anybody behind, not this time. My glare works because none of them bother to argue with me. Good. This time we're doing at least part of this my way. I put Dorna down on the ground, and she stands next to me holding my hand.

"What about my mommy?" She asks.

"She's taking care of some things," Tor replies. "We'll catch up with her later."

"Okay," Dorna says.

My chest constricts, and I bite my lip. What if she never sees her mother again? What if, like my father, she said goodbye without knowing it was a goodbye? Bile rises in my throat, and I have to force myself not to say what's on my mind. It won't do any good.

"We can't stay here," Tor says. "Silas knows where I plan to open the crossing. I'm sure he'll meet us there."

I stare at him, trying to measure the truth of his words. Is he placating me? No, I think he's being honest. I don't think there's a dishonest bone in Tor's body.

"Okay," I agree. "Lead the way."

Tor leads and I take position right behind him. The tunnels are wide enough for two abreast here but ahead the wall juts out, narrowing. It's going to be easiest to go single file. These are rough tunnels, barely formed. We have to pick our way through rubble on the ground. As our ragtag group makes its way through twisting tunnels, the chitter of rats echoes off the stone walls. We're invading their territory.

The lights of the rebel base grow dim. The sigils that Nathaniel put on my arms brighten, casting a soft, silvery glow. It's not intense, but it's enough so that I can see to walk. Nathaniel activates his own sigils, which are much brighter and cast enough light for everyone.

I keep telling myself that I'll see Silas again. It's only a matter of time. He'll be fine.

Except, what if he's not?

I told myself the same things after my Dad disappeared. Over and over I would tell myself he'd come soon, but he never did, not even after years went by.

No, this is different. Silas will come back. I have to believe it. I believe that my Dad will come back too. Sometimes things take time. In that case, we wait. Silas will be fine.

Suddenly, Tor's back is no longer in front of me, and I'm falling forward as my foot steps down onto nothing. Pinwheeling my arms, I try to catch myself, but it's too late. I'm falling. The one foot on solid ground slips too, and I'm sliding down into an open hole. Strong hands grip my shoulders and I'm jerked out of the free fall. Efram pulls me up and against him.

"Why weren't you watching where you're going! You wandered off and nearly got yourself killed," he growls.

His face is so close we're almost touching. His lips tremble and I want to kiss them. His arms around my waist tighten, pulling me closer, and my body molds against his. I relax against him, rising onto my toes....

"Ahem," Rafe clears his throat loudly, jerking me out of the moment.

I feel their eyes burning against my skin. The tension in the energy flow between all of us is intense. Uncomfortably intense. Shuddering, I step away from Efram.

"Thanks," I say, focusing on the ground.

I'd walked right into a hole that I should have seen, if I'd been paying any attention at all. Obviously, I wasn't. Consumed by thoughts of my Dad, I almost screwed everything up, again.

"We should... continue," Efram says, his voice husky and tight.

"Yeah," I agree.

Damn, this is getting out of control. The attraction I feel for all these men is crazy, wrong, and yet so damn right. What in the hell am I doing? How do I, of all the girls in the world, deserve this?

Get a grip Aviella! Focus.

Pushing aside the spinning desires, fantasies, and distractions, I focus on watching where I put my feet. If nothing else, I can at least avoid the obvious pitfalls, even if I can't sidestep the ones in my relationships with my protectors. Huh, good one, self, high five.

"Here," Tor says at last.

"We have to wait," I say. "Silas will be here soon."

The men exchange a look, and I know they think I'm crazy, but I don't care. They have to understand that I care about each of them deeply. I can't leave Silas behind.

"Aviella," Efram says.

"No," I say. "We're not leaving him behind."

Efram frowns and looks at Rafe. Rafe puts his hands up and shrugs, obviously unwilling to argue.

"We don't have long," Tor says. "Every moment, the Dragons' forces come closer. If they're too close, they will stop us before I can get the portal for the crossing open."

My heart pounds. I know he's right, they're all right. It doesn't matter. I can't leave him behind. There has to be a way I can make this work. The tension builds as the seconds tick by. Dorna grips her dad's hand tight, and looking at her brings back memories. Unwanted, unneeded memories of the last time I saw my dad. This world is a mess.

"Okay," I say, making a hard decision. "Open the crossing."

Footsteps echo through the tunnel. Somebody is running. My skin tingles as magic rises, and everyone turns and takes on defensive positions.

Silas runs around the corner and skids to a stop. Everyone breathes a collective sigh of relief.

"Did you doubt me?" he asks, smiling.

"Not for a moment," Rafe says.

"You should all be gone already. They've already broken into the underground. It won't be long before they find you here," Silas says.

"It was decided we should wait for you," Efram says, glancing at me.

Thanks, Efram, appreciate the back up there. I smile and shrug. Silas's steely eyes stare, and he looks grim.

"There's no time," he says. "You have to go now. Tor, open the crossing."

Tor doesn't waste any time, he steps over to the wall and pulls out a piece of chalk. He draws designs in a circle. I haven't seen these before, but they look familiar. They make my blood pulse, and a chill runs down my spine. Once he finishes drawing them, he pulls a key out of his pocket, and presses it against the wall in the center of the sigils that he's drawn. The glyphs flare to life, glowing with a golden light that pulses. They flash brightly, then the wall fades and we're looking into a brightly lit tunnel that appears to be made of swirling light.

"Just like everything in this new world, the crossing point isn't peril-free," Tor says turning to face us all. "You must all be careful."

"We need to go, now" Nathaniel says.

"I'm going to go delay the Dragons," Silas says.

"No," I say.

"Aviella, this is the way it has to be. I'll catch up with you later in your journey."

My chest constricts. It feels like something is squeezing my heart tight. I don't want him to go. It's dangerous. I'm afraid I'll never see him again.

"We're not going either," Gavin says, with the other three mages flanking him. "Our charge right now is Dorna."

Tor's head jerks around, and his eyes widen.

"What?" he asks, shock in his voice and eyes.

"She's special," Killian says, "she has to be protected."

"No, you can't take her," he argues.

Luca smiles and puts an arm on Tor's arm. The fight drains out of him.

"We'll talk more," Killian says to him.

"You can't all leave!" I exclaim, throwing my hands up in the air.

"Hey, what are we?" Rafe asks, ribbing me.

"You know what I mean," I say, waving a hand through

the air. "The damn Dragons are coming, they're not going to let you guys off easy."

"We'll be gone," Gavin says, his eyes taking in Tor and Dorna as well.

"I'll be fine," Silas says.

I hate this. Hate it with a deep burning passion I can't even begin to put into words, but they're right. I know they are, and that makes it even more bitter. Swallowing my pride and upset the best I can, I nod.

"Fine," I huff, crossing my arms over my chest. "If any of you die, I'll never forgive you."

"I'm fairly sure Silas can't die," Rafe jests.

"My point stands," I reply.

"Noted," Silas says, nodding with a half-smile playing across his lips.

Lips that I'd love to kiss. Screw it, I'm doing what I want. I step up to him, rise on my toes, and plant a kiss before anyone can react. I hear Rafe snort behind me. I throw my arms around Silas's neck and continue pressing my lips against his, even though they're stiff and unyielding as he tries to resist. That only lasts for a moment before he gives himself over to my kiss. I don't let it go on for more than a few seconds before I step back and give him one last glare.

"I mean it, if anything happens to you, I'll never forgive you," I order.

Turning without another word, I walk past Rafe, Efram, and Nathaniel, then step into the crossing-point tunnel. I go down a few feet before turning back around and looking.

"Are we doing this or what?" I ask.

I don't wait for an answer before I start walking again.

CHAPTER EIGHT

*T*he flickering light of the tunnel swirls around us, creating a kaleidoscope effect that we're walking through. I feel heavy. Every step is an effort as I leave behind people I care about. Is this what my life is really going to be like? Constantly leaving someone behind? Bringing danger to those foolish enough to invite me into their homes?

Rafe comes up beside me and takes my hand. It's a warm and friendly gesture for which I'm thankful. The sick pit in my stomach eases, and I'm able to focus more in the moment.

My thoughts turn to Dorna and what she had said about breaking through time. Did she mean this crossing tunnel? The crossing tunnel, being a magical creation as it is, is kind of like that. It bends time and space to bring to places closer together. I hadn't thought of that aspect of it.

A low moan pulls me out of my thoughts. Tightening my grip on Rafe's hand I look around. The hair on my arms stands on end. There's a strange energy to the air. Something isn't right, but I can't put my finger on what. As I cast my gaze around trying to figure out what is bothering me, I notice Nathaniel glaring at Rafe's and my joined hands. The moment I see it, he looks away, but not before I feel his need to be the one protecting me. It's palpable. I try to catch his eye, but he doesn't even glance at me again. He pushes past the two of us to take the lead.

An empty ache forms in my chest. It's so hard trying to balance all these men's attention. I don't want to hurt any of them. I care deeply about every single one. There must be some kind of an art to this that I don't get yet. I hope I'll figure it out before it's too late.

The moaning grows louder, and I realize it's echoing through the tunnel. Staring at the walls, I see something is moving behind the swirling colors. No, not something, some things. There are some kind of creatures back there, pressing against the wall, pounding on it and trying to break through. My stomach clenches as cold ice fills my veins. It's so wrong, unnatural, it makes my skin crawl.

As Nathaniel pushes ahead the creature reaches through the wall. It's a skeletal arm followed by an even uglier face, a horrid, demonic-looking thing. Nathaniel barely spares it a glance and presses his hand against its head. There's an instant of blinding white light, and the creature lets out a harsh, rattling shriek, its death cries echoing around us.

It strikes me then that we're surrounded by these things on all sides of the tunnel. A cold chill runs down my spine as I get it. They're after our energy, they feed on magic, and Nathaniel's display of power drew them to us. I have no doubt if they were to break through, we would be in trouble.

"This isn't good," Efram says, pressing in close behind us.

Another hand reaches through, grabbing at Nathaniel. I yelp involuntarily. Something reaches through from the other side and grabs Rafe. He lets go of my hand and turns to deal with it. As I turn to see what he's fighting, something grabs me, pulling me against the wall. I look over my shoulder, and I'm staring into a symbol.

I'm falling into it, seeing past it, and it pulls me deeper. Eyes are looking at me. Dark, beautiful eyes, yet malevolent. I lose myself in them completely. They're absorbing, intelligent, and so intriguing.

I'm jerked around hard and the eyes are gone. Rafe's hands are on either side of my face. He's barely an inch away, his eyes glowing. He's angry, I feel it as much as I see it. He opens his mouth to say something.

"Look out," Efram yells, interrupting.

Rafe jerks me towards him, spinning me around. A creature reaches through the wall, grabbing for him. He ducks under its waving arms, and Nathaniel steps in, his hands glowing as he slams them against it. It explodes, turning to dust that fills the tunnel making it harder to breathe.

"Run!" Rafe says, pointing down the tunnel.

He doesn't have to tell me twice. More of these things are breaking through. The walls of the tunnel are apparently getting thinner. I run, dodging grasping arms and screaming monsters gnashing teeth as I go. I hear the others behind me but don't pause to look. There's a bright glow straight ahead.

"That's the end of the tunnel," Nathaniel says. "Faster!"

"Yeah," I pant, out of breath.

Three things, there's barely enough parts to call them creatures, fall out of the walls and land on the tunnel in front of me. I slide to a stop, my magic rising. It thrums through my soul.

The things stumble to their feet, shambling at me with reaching arms. They moan, a horrid, empty sound. I bring my arms together and weave them like Nathaniel showed me, to create a blinding light to keep them from reaching me. I hear the boys fighting behind me. I dodge to one side, avoiding a creature. When I clench my fist, my magic pools into them and I feel suddenly powerful. I've done so much shadow sparring, what happens next comes naturally. I punch, but instead of meeting the expected resistance of my fist landing on a thing's face, it keeps on going. The creature's head explodes.

"We have to get out of here," Efram says.

I don't need to be told twice. Having created an opening, I run and leap for the end of the tunnel. As I pass into the opening, everything slows, like I've leaped into a wall of molasses. It clings to me, not wanting to let me go. Finally breaking free, I stumble forward, pinwheeling my arms to catch my balance. Whirling around, I look for my friends. Efram comes through first, moving backwards. He stumbles also as he comes out, followed by Rafe. The tunnel flickers and fades. It's about to close.

"Nathaniel!" I scream.

I see him on the other side, the creatures closing with him. He's about to be surrounded. Determination fills me as I step forward. I'm going in after him. Efram and Rafe grab me from either side.

"Aviella, you can't," Rafe says.

"We're not leaving anybody behind," I shout.

I struggle against them, but when it comes to brute strength, I'm outgunned. They hold me back.

Nathaniel's wings appear spreading wide, he glows with a bright white light. It flashes blindingly bright leaving after-shock effects on my retina. I'm blind and dependent on sound.

"Nathaniel!" I scream.

He has to be okay. I'm not going to lose any of them. My heart pounds and it's hard to breathe. Something pops, a loud sound, and in my heart, I know it's the tunnel closing, but I don't know if Nathaniel made it out though. Darkness encloses us, so pitch black I can't see my hand in front of my face even after the flash-effect fades.

"Nathaniel?" I ask, hearing the tremble in my own voice.

"I'm here," Nathaniel answers, after a tense moment.

I breathe a sigh of relief.

"You had us for a second there," Efram says.

"I had to make sure she made it out," Nathaniel says, voice subdued.

My heart skips a beat as my chest constricts. He'd die for me if it was needed. There's no doubt or question of it. It's romantic and frightening both. Who am I to deserve such dedication? Rafe grabs me by my shoulders and pulls me around to face him.

"What the—"

His eyes glow golden, illuminating the fury on his face.

"Never!" he says, gripping my shoulders tighter.

"Never what?" I shout, anger flashing at the way he's handling me.

"Never look into the symbol. Never!" he says.

"Why?" I ask. There's something in his energy, the way he feels.

"You must not, ever—it's evil. When you look into it, it reads you… and worse."

"What is it?" I ask.

Suddenly it hits me. Fear. He's afraid. His fear flutters against me like wings dancing along my awareness, but I feel it sliding into me too. My stomach drops and cold sweat drenches my back. Rafe, afraid. I've never felt anything like it. He's hiding it behind the anger, but I've no doubt I'm right. Rafe shakes his head and looks away.

"Rafe?" Efram asks.

"What do you know about it?" I ask, probing.

"It's of the hell realms," he says. "None of us need to go poking around it, not right now. Not ever. Those forces have grown hungry for power, hungrier. It's a less-happy place than before, if that is even possible."

Something in his words makes the cold chill deeper.

"Why would the realms…" Efram trails off.

"We should move," Nathaniel interjects.

"What aren't you all saying?" I ask, looking at Rafe and Nathaniel.

The two of them look at each other and shake their heads. Efram watches obviously in as much confusion as I am.

"Nothing," Rafe says. "That's the entirety of the problem, Aviella, we don't know."

I didn't think I could get any colder than I am, but I shiver at his words. The emptiness of not knowing is all consuming. A yawning blackness I could lose myself in.

"Okay," I say, shaking myself. "All right then. Well, I guess we worry about that later for later."

"Good idea," Rafe says.

Nathaniel gestures and the sigils decorating his arms take on a familiar silvery glow, illuminating the area immediately around us. We're standing in what looks like an abandoned tunnel. The walls are rough cut and barely finished. Even the floor is rough, unusual for tunnels in my experience with Bunker life. Efram goes to the wall and places a hand over an area covered with pockmarks. He jerks his hand back as soon as he touches it.

"We should move," Efram says, backing away from the wall.

Nathaniel doesn't need more encouragement and leads the way.

"What was it?" I ask Efram, moving up next to him as we walk.

"I'm not sure," he says.

"Great, well focus on what we do know, right?" I say.

"Yeah," he says, forcing a smile.

The darkness around us is oppressive. The air itself seems heavy, like a massive tragedy happened here. The hair on my arms stands on end and won't lie down. That creepy sense of being watched that makes the skin on back of your neck crawl doesn't quit. I keep looking around to see if we're being followed, but there's nothing but shadows, dancing around the silvery light of Nathaniel's sigils.

The air smells of sickness and decay. An oppressive odor that clings to the insides of my nostrils. It's disgusting, and my stomach is sour because of it. Everything feels wrong. It's all strange, but nothing I can put a finger on. It's a feeling. A sick, nasty feeling. The steady silver light doesn't illuminate much beyond our small group as we make our way through the tunnel. None of us are talking as we walk. Eventually, I have no clue how long, there's a light up ahead. It's not bright, but it's the only change in quite a while. As it grows brighter, the shapes come clear as we approach a door. The door is a metal thing with one of those wheel locks like you'd find on a submarine. A small window made of thick glass lets the light on the other side into the dark tunnel.

Rafe walks up to it and takes the wheel. It doesn't move when he tries to turn it. He plants his feet and strains, and it screeches, barely moving. Nathaniel steps up with him, and together they're able to turn it. It's loud as it turns and ends with a loud metallic clang. It scrapes open taking both of them to force it. A burning odor wafts out and assaults my nose. I sneeze in response—it's awful—but I can't decide if it's worse than the odor in the tunnel or not. Rafe and Nathaniel lead the way through the door, and I follow with Efram. On the other side, a single light bulb with bare wires running to it hangs from the ceiling casting a flickering, yellow light.

We're in what looks like a waiting room or an entry way. It's a box of sorts. The walls are painted a pale green but it's flaking off leaving bare rust spots all around. There's a door on the far side, similar to the one we just came through. To our left is a doorway covered with a blanket. On the right is a row of rusty lockers.

Sitting next to the lockers is a man who rises to his feet from a rickety stool as we walk in. He looks... off. Something about him isn't right, but I don't know what it is. Like he's not all there, something in his eyes, or the creepy, somehow vacantly fixed smile showing rotting teeth that he gives us. His skin is sallow, his eyes sunken, and his face looks like a skull barely covered with skin. His head is mottled with patches of hair interspersed with liver-brown bald spots. He weaves as he stands, staring.

"Howdy," he says, a southern drawl to his words. "Didn't reckon I'd be seeing anyone today."

I can't tell if his eyes are glowing on their own or reflecting the flickering light. Even his energy feels off, almost wrong, but again it's nothing I can pinpoint. Rafe and Nathaniel stand between him and me, tactically keeping him at bay.

"And you are?" Rafe asks.

"Hunter," he says, holding a thin hand out. "Pleased ta meet ya."

Rafe doesn't take the offered hand.

"Right, well, we need to travel through," Rafe says, looking at the door on the far side of the room.

"Oh, well, you'll need protection in there," he says. "Decontamination first, then you'll need rad suits."

"Rad suits?" Nathaniel asks.

"Oh yeah, if you're going above ground you'll need them," he says, shaking his head. He turns to one side, spits, turns back and grins broadly. "Sum parts tha facility need 'em too."

My stomach turns watching him. He's gross and creepy. What a combination.

"I don't need such protection," Nathaniel says. "And we're

only passing through. Rafe and I will be scouting a path ahead then we'll be out of here."

"Huh," Hunter says. "Well that may be, but you'll still have to decontaminate. It's for the residents you see. Have to take care of them."

The way he says residents makes my skin crawl. He shrugs and stares with his fixed smile.

"Fine," I say, grabbing the bull by the horns. "What do we have to do to decontaminate?"

"Showers are through there," he says. "Scrub *real* good."

It takes all my will to not roll my eyes at the way he emphasizes real. It's lewd giving him a whole new level of gross.

"Aviella-" Efram starts.

"No," I say, shaking my head. "Let's get this over with."

I turn and go through the curtain. There is a row of small shower stalls with opaque plastic sheets covering each of them. Dirty tiles on the floor and walls and a single yellow bulb for illumination in here too. The lighting is enough to make it creepy without the added accents of the pale colors on the walls and the mildew-covered tiles.

The boys follow me in. Nathaniel and Efram look uncomfortably around noticing there is no changing area or any way to gain even a semblance of privacy. Strangely, maybe because I'm broken inside, I'm instantly aroused. Seeing my three men naked, at the same time, sends my thoughts spinning in a totally different direction than the setting should allow. Of course, it's a welcome escape from the reality I'm facing.

"Well," Rafe says, and shrugging, he starts stripping.

Leave it to him to have no shame. Out of instinct, I turn my back and he snorts, loudly. Great Rafe, thanks for that. It's not like this isn't awkward enough.

"Right," Efram says, sighing.

Feeling self-conscious, I slowly undress and grab a towel from a stack by the door. Carefully I do my best not to look at the men as they undress. Okay, I can't help a peek, but it's only a quick glance. I have to know and... damn. They're all very... well-endowed. And ripped. So damn ripped. Swallowing hard I hurry into the stall and pull the curtain closed. The water is cold, and I yelp.

"Aviella?" Efram asks.

"Fine, it's colder than I expected."

"Ah," Efram responds.

THE SOUND OF RUNNING WATER ECHOES OFF THE TILES. Grabbing soap, I try to focus. Efram is in the stall next to mine, which makes it hard. It'd be nice if he were in the stall with me. Scrubbing my back, touching me, leaning in for a kiss...

Stop it!

I'm nuts. There could not possibly be a less sexy situation to be in than this, and here I am thinking about... no. Stop. Seriously. Hurrying, I finish scrubbing and shut off the water. I wring my hair out, grab a towel, and wrap it around myself. I take a deep, cleansing breath, then step outside the small stall.

The moment I do, Hunter is right there, too damn close, and my skin crawls as I stumble back to keep him out of my personal space. His eyes are glued to my chest, staring at the edge of my towel, which makes him even creepier. He has that fixed, crazy smile on his face, and there is something in his eyes. My magic swells, creating a tingling sensation down my arms and legs. Clenching my teeth, I seize control of it before it lashes out. I really don't like this guy. Something is off about him.

"Sorry," he says, grin not fading. "Thought you might need some more towels."

He holds out a stack of towels in front of him, but his eyes never come up to meet mine.

"We're fine," I snap. "Thanks."

"I'll just leave them over here," he says, turning and putting them on the bench.

The curtains over the showers rattle almost as one, and all three of my men step out. Nathaniel and Efram have towels draped around their waists in at least a modicum of modesty but not Rafe. My cheeks burn hot as I get an eyeful of his impressive manhood, which he has no qualms about showing off.

"Thank you for the towels," Nathaniel says, stepping between Hunter and me. "We'll be out shortly."

"Right," Hunter nods with forceful enthusiasm. "Glad to hear it."

He turns and walks out. I let out a breath I didn't realize I'd been holding. My heart slows, but knowing that Rafe is full-on, out-and-about I stare at the ceiling, pointedly ignoring his nudity.

"Rafe," Nathaniel snaps.

"Yup?" he asks, either feigning or actually being innocent.

"A towel, please," Nathaniel says.

"Oh, right," Rafe says, his voice annoyingly teasing.

My cheeks must be fire red. They're burning so hot it feels like my skin is going to melt off. Rafe grabs a towel and wraps himself. My heart slowly returns to a normal pace, and the four of us look at each other.

"Yeah," I say to fill the silence. "I'm going to dress really quick."

Nathaniel and Efram turn their back without a word. Rafe grins broadly and waits. I arch an eyebrow, but before I say anything, Efram grabs his shoulder and forces him to turn around. Rafe moans loudly but doesn't try to peek while I dress. Once I'm dressed, I tell the guys so they can dress too, and I walk out the door to let them do so in private.

When I leave there, Hunter is perched back on his rickety stool, staring at me as soon as I enter the room. He rocks forward, the stool making a clack as it hits the ground. My skin tingles, magic rising, ready for anything, but he doesn't move. A few minutes later, the boys rejoin me.

"Okay, well, now you're all decontaminated, I can let you through to the registration room," Hunter says, standing up. "You'll need these."

He opens a locker next to him and pulls out bright yellow hazard suits. He hands them to each of us, and we put them on over our clothes. Nathaniel doesn't bother putting one on, snorting when Hunter hands it to him.

"Suit yourself," Hunter says, walking to the door opposite the one we came in. He turns the wheel and the door swings silently open. "Bunker Registration is down the hall. They'll help you find a place to stay on the other side."

"Thanks," I say, stepping through the door, glad to be quit of him.

Hunter shuts the door behind us, and the clang of the metal bars sliding into place echoes around us. This is a connection tunnel we're in, so we walk ahead until it comes to another heavy door. On the other side of that door is a small room with a similar door on the far side.

Safety signs on the walls illustrate that you can take off the suits here. After we close the door we came through, we lose the suits, hanging them on pegs on the wall. It seems strange because I've seen movies with rooms like this, and there is usually some kind of water or smoke stuff that washes away whatever the suit was protecting you from before you take it off. At least a rush of air or something. Nothing happens though.

A thin woman sitting behind a desk looks up when we enter. There's a haunted look to her eyes, which part of me instantly blames on her being even this close to Hunter. She nods as we step into the room, smacks her lips, then shakes her head.

"How long?" she asks.

"A night, at the most," Nathaniel answers.

"Go down that hall, look to the right, and there's an open bunk room. You can share it."

She stares down at her hands behind the desk, ignoring us, so we head down the hall she half-pointed at and walk until we find an open room on the right. There are three sets of bunks in the room and a couple of small chests along with a sink and toilet in the corner. It's very basic, but at least it's a place to rest.

"We need to plot our path. We shouldn't stay here any longer than absolutely necessary," Nathaniel says.

"Right," Rafe says. "Nate and I will be back."

"Are you sure it's safe?" I ask.

"Of course not!" Rafe exclaims. "There will be loads of danger and adventures. Mighty tales to woo you with on our return."

He grins mischievously until Nathaniel jabs him in the ribs with an elbow.

"Ow," Rafe says.

He glares at Nathaniel. Nathaniel doesn't dignify him with response. I laugh.

"Why don't you wait for morning?" I ask. "Going at night seems like a terrible idea."

"We need to find a safe path, and if it comes down to it and Rafe has to use his Crossing Key, we need to know the safest place to use it," Nathaniel answers.

"And the wooing," Rafe adds, grinning. "Don't forget the wooing."

Nathaniel glares at him, but it doesn't slow Rafe down in the least. I can't argue with their logic, well, outside the wooing bit, of course. I want to, sure, but Nathaniel's right. It's stupid to not be prepared. My stomach is sour, and my skin feels icky through and through. I know it's because of Hunter. I look over my shoulder back towards where we left him.

"I'll be here," Efram says, seeing my glance.

"Don't you... feel it?" I ask, unsure how to put the feeling into words.

"Yeah," Efram says.

"That is one weird dude," Rafe says.

"There is something off about him," Nathaniel says. "But that only reinforces what we must do. We cannot stay here."

"Fine," I say, shuddering. "It's just... that guy could be the star monster of a late-night horror show, you know?"

"He might have been," Rafe says, unhelpfully.

"Rafe!" I exclaim.

Rafe grins as he walks over. He grabs my shoulders and stares into my eyes, his eyes serious for once.

"Nothing," he says, his voice solemn. "And I mean nothing, will happen to you. He would have to come through all of us first, and that is not happening."

The weight of his words, heavy with intention and unspoken emotions, layers across me, holding me down and lifting me up at the same time. The three men look at me as the air becomes charged with anticipation. Their energy weaves into mine, intertwining, twisting together, too similar to the way my fantasies have imagined our bodies. Swallowing hard, I nod, my lips trembling, wanting more, but I can't possibly ask that of them.

"We'll be back soon," Nathaniel says, breaking the moment. "Get some rest."

They leave without another word, though both Rafe and

Nathaniel cast a last lingering glance at me before they leave the room. Efram and I are alone. There's a moment of awkward silence as we look at each other, then my belly grumbles loudly. Efram chuckles and shakes his head.

"We should find some food," he says.

"Yeah," I agree, glad to have something to do besides stare at his perfect lips, strong jaw, and his stunning eyes.

He steps forward and takes my hand, but as he does, a scream resounds through the walls, causing cold chills to run down my arms. I look around wildly, trying to find the source of the noise. It doesn't sound human. Efram pushes me behind him, protectively.

There's a moment of silence, and then a roar echoes off the walls. The screeching scream comes again as if in answer to the roar. Efram and I exchange a look, and he shakes his head.

"Welcome to Wormwood," he says.

"Great," I say, shaking my head and steeling my nerves. "Seems like the perfect Apocalypse vacation spot."

Efram chuckles. "Yeah. Courtesy of the former United States government and their experiments."

"Okay, well let's find food," I say.

We head out into the hallway together and wander around. The sounds continue until it's almost white noise. Although every once in a while, one of them is particularly loud causing me to jump.

Eventually we come to a kitchenette/dining area. It's empty but lots of picnic-style tables are set around ready for use. One wall is lined with machines. Old-style vending machines. Oddly, they're actually stocked.

"I don't have any coins," I say, looking the machines over.

"I think I do," Efram says, digging through his pockets.

He pulls out handfuls of odds and ends and digs through it, managing to find some coins. Enough that we can each get some food. He inserts the coins and the food drops, making a loud clatter. I look around to see if we've attracted any attention, but we're still alone.

I open the receptacle and take out the dried meats before popping them into a microwave, hitting the buttons to warm them up. When I turn to say something to Efram, I jump, because a woman is standing there. I don't know where she came from, but she jerks back and raises her arms protectively. At the same time, there is a particularly loud roar that almost makes the walls shake, and all three of us jump.

"Hello," I say to the newcomer, holding out a hand and smiling, trying to be friendly. "I'm Aviella."

She barely meets my eyes, hers keep darting away. When she reaches to take my hand, hers is trembling. Efram, for his part, is keeping his distance.

"They won't quiet down," she says. "You get used to it after a while."

"Thank you," I reply. "That's very kind of you to tell us."

She nods meekly, then turns and walks away. She disappears through a door, and I turn back to Efram.

"What was that about?" I ask.

"I'm not sure," he says.

The microwave dings alerting us to our food being ready. Tossing the packages from hand to hand to avoid getting burned, I put them down on one of the tables where Efram and I sit. The smell of the meat when I open the package, even if it's probably some kind of proto-meat, makes my mouth water. I dig in with relish.

Efram eats slower, and his energy probes at me. He's trying to be subtle, and I know there was a time I probably wouldn't have noticed. My sensitivity is increasing.

"Just ask," I say, at last.

"What?" he asks, eyes widening.

"Whatever it is you're trying to figure out," I say, swallowing a mouthful of food. "Just ask."

"Stop worrying," he says, arching an eyebrow.

"I'm not worried," I say.

It's not exactly a lie. I wouldn't call it worry myself anyway. Efram arches an eyebrow as he slowly chews his food. He continues watching, silent, waiting for me to say more. I try to hold out. I know what he's doing, using silence to encourage me to talk.

"I'm a little overwhelmed," I say, folding at last. "And a whole lot of creeped out. In truth though, I haven't had time to worry."

"Don't be," he says, filled with confidence and certainty. "We're going to figure this out."

"How can you be so sure?" I ask. "There are so many moving parts. We don't even know who's after me."

He places a hand over mine, and my skin warms at his touch. We lock eyes with each other and our energy melds into one.

"I promise you," he says. "We're going to figure out who's trying to snatch you. We will find your father. We have a lot of allies, and all of us are focused on helping you."

"And find out who's waiting for me when I break through time?"

"Yes, that too," he smiles.

Something about his confidence communicates to me, filling me with certainty, and I know, on some level, he's right. If I don't believe that, what do I have? I sigh and dig back into my meal.

CHAPTER NINE

*O*n the bunk, I toss and turn fitfully. Sleep eludes me. Every time I think I'm about to doze off, I see the image of that symbol floating in front of me. I do my best not to focus on it. I'm afraid of it since Rafe's warning.

It's not like my magic has done any good against anything that has had the symbol. Maybe that's what's worrying me. Worry. Dammit, maybe Efram is right. I guess I am worried. It's not like there isn't good cause! Everything is going to hell. Everywhere we go, destruction follows in my wake.

Images of Bunker E247 drift past. All those people, lost, because of me. I put them in harm's way. The things that are after me don't care who they hurt. That's a scary thought.

In the bunk below, Efram's steady breathing tells me he's asleep. Stabbing jealousy pierces through my heart. What I wouldn't give to be asleep right now too! I think I'd feel better if Rafe and Nathaniel were back. I'm worried about them too. I know they can take care of themselves, but it doesn't lessen my concern.

I roll on my side, take hold of the pillow, and pull it tight around my head, trying to drown out the constant sounds that echo through the halls. Closing my eyes tightly, I try to will myself to sleep. Eventually it works.

A loud screeching sound jerks me awake, and I sit straight up in bed, whacking my head on the low ceiling.

"Ow!" I yell. "Damn it."

"Are you okay?" Efram asks, appearing next to the bunk.

"What is that infernal sound," I grouch, shoving my fingers in my ears to block out the noise.

Efram looks around. Outside the opening to our bunk, people walk down the hallway, heading toward something.

"It seems to be an alarm," Efram says.

"Hey," Hunter says, appearing in the door. "Y'all need to get to the assignments. You stay here y'all gotta pay."

Efram and I exchange a look before I slide off the bed and we join the crowd walking down the hall. Eventually, we're all in the dining area we found last night. Three people are set up at a table in front of the vending machines. Everyone forms lines in front of the table and shuffles their way forward, one at a time. When they reach the front, they're handed a card, which they take and then wander off.

Unsure what to do, Efram and I join the line. We reach the front at last, and I'm handed a card. I look at it and arch an eyebrow. It has a room number and says "walls."

"Excuse me," I say, to the person who handed me the card. "What does this mean?"

She rolls her eyes and sigh heavily, as if I just placed the weight of the world upon her.

"It's your cleaning duty," she says.

"Oh," I say.

I glance over my shoulder at Efram and shrug. He steps forward and gets his own card. We compare them and luckily, by some happy chance, we've been assigned to the same room, but his says floors.

I notice Hunter standing to one side watching the

proceedings. He has his arms crossed and that same fixed, empty grin on his face. Every time I see him, my skin crawls. I can't imagine having to deal with him on a regular basis. Worse, he seems to be paying particular attention to me. Great, just what I need, a creepy fanboy.

Efram and I wander around trying to find the room we've been assigned to clean. It takes us a little time, but we manage locate it. A young man is already in there working when we arrive. He turns at our entrance and smiles.

"Hey, there," he says. "I'm Cordy."

"Hi Cordy, I'm Aviella" I say. "This is Efram."

We all shake hands and then set about our work. Cordy and I are both on wall scrubbing, and he seems to make a point of being very close to me. He seems nice enough, and he makes casual conversation while we work. It helps the time go by.

"Have you seen them?" he asks suddenly.

"Who?" I ask.

"*Them*," he whispers, emphasizing the word while his eyes go wide.

I shake my head in confusion. He drops the sponge in his hand and grabs both my arms gripping them tight. It's almost hard enough to hurt. He leans in really close, and I smell his breakfast on his breath.

"You should leave, now," he hisses. "Before the haunts get you."

"What haunts?" I ask.

"All the people who died," he whispers.

Staring into his eyes, I see madness. While he seemed nice at first, it must've been a cover. There's very little at home here.

"I don't know what you mean," I reply.

"Everyone who died here is stuck in a no-man's-land.

They're trying to break back through. They get really restless at night."

The worst part is, even if he is crazy, his words might be true. I've seen too much to doubt anything weird without further proof it's not for real. It is the Apocalypse out there.

It draws my mind back to the symbol. An image of it flows through my thoughts, but I try to push it away. I'm worried that thinking about it can trigger the effects Rafe warned of. Especially since my magic has been next-to-useless at fending off anything bearing it. I have to find something I can do to be effective. I can't be this vulnerable.

"Okay," I say, answering Cordy. "Thank you for the warning."

He nods enthusiastically, picks his sponge back up, and returns to scrubbing the wall. I go back to finishing the chore I was assigned as well. The rest of our time together passes uneventfully. When we're done, Efram and I are left alone again.

"Maybe we should explore a bit," Efram says. "We might learn something useful."

"Yeah," I agree.

Anything to keep my mind off the symbol and of what's going on with Rafe and Nathaniel. Doing something with our time is better than sitting around doing nothing—by far.

CHAPTER TEN

EFRAM

*S*he veils her emotions, putting a brave face over everything. It's admirable and I appreciate it. But no matter what kind of face she puts on, she can't hide what's really going on with her, not from me. I feel her concerns. It pervades her energy and pounds against me like the waves of the ocean. Almost it makes me feel like a lighthouse trying to hold strong amidst the raging storm of her emotions.

If the intensity keeps going up she'll end up with a headache at the very least. I have to find a way to help her relax. I should be able to do something. I know she's not sleeping, and that's probably the biggest part of the problem. At night I hear her tossing and turning, and sometimes she cries out.

I wish she would talk to me. Maybe then I could figure out how to help. She's kept herself withdrawn. I'm sure she thinks she's being brave, protecting those around her, because that's the way she is. It's part of what I love and admire about her. Her heart is bigger than anybody I've ever met.

"So where do you want to go?" Aviella asks.

"I thought we'd would go a little deeper into this Bunker. See what else there is here," I reply.

She nods, pursing her lips.

"Yeah," she says. "There's something off about this entire place."

"This was all part of the Wormwood facility," I say. "It's where the government created most of the monsters that broke loose early on."

As if in response to my words, another one of the loud screeches echoes through the halls. Something scratches at the walls on the other side of our bunk. Aviella jumps and looks around. It's a common sound, though it hasn't been this close before.

"I'll be really glad to leave this place behind," she mutters.

"We'll need hazmat suits," I say. "Hunter says some of the areas are still dangerous."

Aviella nods. Dark circles are forming under eyes, confirming my suspicion of her lack of sleep. Maybe tonight I'll drain a bit of her energy off, that should help her to get some rest. Of course, if she ever found out I did it, she'd be pissed as hell.

I debate the merits of such an action while we dress in the protective suits. I still haven't come to a decision when were ready to move through to the next section of the Bunker.

We go through a decontamination room, and on the other side is another rough set of tunnels. There are long scratch marks down the walls. Aviella walks over and touches them. She looks over her shoulder arching an eyebrow.

"I don't think we want to know," I answer her unspoken question. "Let's just hope we don't run into it."

She nods, and we walk side-by-side through the tunnels. The tunnel opens up and becomes smoother as we walk along. It isn't long before we enter the next section of the

Wormwood facility. The area begins to look familiar, and then it hits me—I've been here before. This is one of the experimentation areas.

The same pale green, sick-looking tiles decorate the walls. Flickering fluorescent lights cast a dim illumination that doesn't seem to reach the corners. Massive cages are set around the walls interspersed with heavy chains. Once-sterile metal tables dominate the middle of the rooms, covered in stains. I can only imagine the source of those stains.

A roar echoes through the room. Aviella jumps and lands in a crouch looking around wildly for the source. The howl continues, growing louder, the sound of it bouncing off the tile walls. When it finally fades my ears are ringing.

"What in the holy hell was that?" Aviella asks, her voice echoing strangely through the hazmat suit.

I shake my head and swallow hard. Memories come without warning. I've heard that sound before, and I hope we don't run into it. This may have been a very bad idea.

"A mammoth," I say.

"What in the hell is a mammoth?" she asks, rising from her defensive crouch.

"Something I hope we never run into," I reply.

"I take it you've seen one," she says.

I nod, the memory consuming my thoughts, pulling me into it.

"Yeah," I say. "A few years ago, I guided a group of survivors through here. This was back when the rails through this area were still working. We were supposed to just pass through, never intending to stop. Something tore up the rails, forcing us to abandon the car.

"We unloaded here, in this area. I'm certain now it was a planned attack. The first thing we heard was that monster, and then it was on us. No one with me had any fighting ability."

Aviella places a hand on my arm. She looks up into my eyes through the plastic plates separating us, our protective gear. I stare into her eyes, losing myself in her. It helps push away the darkness of my memories.

"What happened?" she asks.

"I tried," I say, swallowing hard.

Aviella nods. She tightens her grip on my arm and touches the side of the headgear covering my face.

"Go on," she says, encouraging me.

"It was the worst thing I've experienced. I lost all of them. I fought with everything I had. My magic wasn't strong enough to save them. The mammoth… I hope you never see one."

"You did what you had to do," she reassures me.

"Yeah," I agree. "That's the problem. I survived; they didn't."

"I understand," she says. "I still think about Bunker E247. What else could I have done?"

Her eyes drop away from mine. The sadness and the loss are palpable in her energy. This is the source, as much as anything, of her worry. It's a testament to her heart. So many people still alive at this point in the Apocalypse care about nothing but themselves. Not Aviella. She's always worrying about everybody around her, and not just those closest to her.

My hearts pounds and my breath is coming in ragged gasps. I can't ignore my arousal. My desire for her is both physical and spiritual.

No, I can't give in. No matter how much I want to. I know I'm bound to her. There's no question about that. When she looks up at me, her lips flushed, it takes every effort of my will to not pull her into my arms. No matter the suits protecting and separating us I want to, take her. Claim her, but more than that I want her to claim me, physically to match the way she has marked my soul.

I turn away. I can't look at her and resist my baser urges too. Having her bonded to me as a companion is safe. If she goes any further, I don't know where we would end up. It could have consequences, ones I'm not sure I'm ready to face. I'm afraid I would lose myself in her.

Give it more time, I reassure myself. It's what I've been doing or at least trying to do. It's just been so damn hard.

We continue exploring this section of the tunnels. It helps to focus on something else, anything besides her. She's so damn beautiful. I didn't know that anyone, anywhere, at any time could make a hazmat suit look attractive, but Aviella pulls it off.

This section is deserted as far as we can tell. We find no other survivors. Turning a corner we come to a dining area with vending machines. None of the product inside seems to be any good. We continue the explorations, hoping to find something useful. My main idea behind this was giving her something else to focus on besides her worries. Get her out of her head a bit. At least that part seems to be working.

"What do you think is over there?" she asks, pointing to a door that leads into a dark area.

"No idea," I say, shrugging. "How about we find out?"

I don't want to admit to her that I'm nervous. I don't want to run into one of those mammoths. Aviella is powerful and I don't doubt that together we could handle it, but why take the risk? The memories of my last encounter haunt me. So many lives lost, and their blood is on my hands.

Aviella is fearless, as usual. She walks towards the darkness beyond the door and I follow. I'm enthralled with her. I can't tell her no, and I know it. I'm hers to command, even if I will only admit that to myself. Realizing how entwined I am with her is frightening in its own way. I've never been dependent on another like I am her. The closest was my sister and losing her was almost the end of me. If anything happened to Aviella, I don't know what I would do. The thought is so dark, my stomach turns and I have to push it away.

The light from the previous room casts weird shadows into the one we enter. Hydroponic tables line the walls, growing food, but something is off. The growth lights aren't casting light but there are plants growing on the tables. They look like food. Lettuces, tomatoes, cauliflower and other items but how are they growing without light? Aviella walks over to one of the tables, moving slowly, and I follow her. She feels it too, I know. Everything about this area is wrong, like so much of Wormwood. Wrongness pervades the whole place, creating a constant assault on my awareness.

"How?" she mutters, leaning over the table to look at the growing plants.

"I don't know," I say, joining her and looking closer.

"It's wrong," she observes. "It *feels* off."

She passes a hand over the growing table, and I would swear that the plants vibrate as her hand passes over them. It's creepy, and a further testament to the wrongness of what's happening here.

"We should be careful about what we eat while we're here," I say.

"You think?" she asks, sarcastically.

There's a sound behind us and we turn to look. Hunter walks into the room. His wild eyes stare at us but not from behind the protective gear of a hazmat suit because he's not wearing one.

"Y'all need to get out of here," he says. "This area is off limits right now."

Aviella and I exchange a glance before nodding.

"Yeah, no problem," I agree.

He steps to one side of the door letting us pass. He has his arms crossed over his chest, and despite the feelings of anger and upset rolling off him, he has that same crazy, fixed smile on his face. He stares as we leave and head back the way we came. After we've walked a short distance, I look over my shoulder and see no sign of Hunter.

"That guy can't be human," Aviella says.

She holds up her arm and points at the badge there that indicates the radiation levels. It glows a deep red, which means no human can survive in this area.

"He's definitely something... more," I agree. "I have no idea what though."

Aviella nods. "Yeah. I hope Nathaniel and Rafe are home soon. I'm ready to leave."

We make our way back to the decontamination chamber, where we take off our suits and then head back to the bunk we were assigned. It's been a long day and we're hungry, so we stop by the commissary. When we walk in, there are a handful of others eating.

I buy some food from the vending machines, carefully picking stuff that looks like it's prepackaged only. Once I pop it out of the microwave, I take it to the table where Aviella is sitting waiting. The resident who was talking to her before, Cordy I believe his name is, is standing before Aviella.

"The haunts always test the new ones. Don't let them into your heads," Cordy says, grinning.

"Thanks," Aviella says, her eyes darting to me.

"No problem," Cordy says. "Just trying to be helpful."

"I appreciate it," Aviella says, taking the food I offer her.

Cordy wanders off, leaving Aviella and me alone.

"What was that?" I ask.

"It's something he's been talking about. He says everyone

who has died here is stuck in a no-man's-land and haunts this place."

"Great," I say. "Because dealing with all the government-experiment creatures wasn't enough."

"Hey, what would our life be if it wasn't exciting all the time," Aviella says with a grin.

CHAPTER ELEVEN

"They should have been back by now," I complain, slamming my hands down onto the bunk.

I've been lying here for what feels like hours, waiting. Since Hunter cut off our explorations, we've been hanging out in the bunk. I'm worried and I'm bored, never a good combination.

"They'll be back soon," Efram answers, his voice reassuring.

"Yeah, but when?" I ask. "We need to get out of here. This place is creepy."

"I know," Efram agrees. "It won't be long, I'm sure."

"Ugh," I grouse.

As if to enhance my desire to no longer be here, there's another long, drawn-out roar filling the hallways and echoing off the walls. I arch an eyebrow at Efram letting the noise affirm my position. Efram shrugs and shakes his head.

"What can we do?" he asks. "You know they have to find a safe path. This is our best option right now. Patience is a virtue."

"Patience? How long have you known me?"

"Right, bad choice of words," Efram replies. "How about we play some cards?"

"Just because I'm agreeing to do this doesn't mean I like it," I say, swinging my legs over the edge of the bunk and jumping to the floor.

"Noted," Efram replies.

He pulls out a deck of cards from one of his pockets and shuffles them. His fingers are deft and quick. I take up my hand that he deals to me and look it over. We play a couple of rounds both of which I win. I suspect he's allowing me to because it doesn't seem like he's trying very hard.

The girl, Mina, walks in with both of her arms loaded with clothing as Efram deals our third hand. She looks around nervously, swallows hard, and motions up and down with her arms.

"Hi," I offer, hoping to reassure her.

She trembles and her eyes dart all around avoiding making contact. She swallows hard and her mouth opens as if she's going to say something, then snaps shut. Another tremor, she nods her head repeatedly, then her mouth opens again.

"Hunter says," she says, her voice quavering, "you should wear these."

She motions with the clothing in her hands then holds them out in front of herself.

"Wear them where?" I ask, confusion rising.

It doesn't look like protective suits that she's carrying, hell one of them looks like a dress.

"You're to come to dinner," she says, her voice still trembling.

Efram and I exchange a glance. Going to dinner with Hunter is the last thing in the world I would want to do, even if we hadn't stumbled across the weird hydroponic garden.

The fact that he wants us to eat food here, that doesn't bode well.

"I don't think we're going to be hungry," Efram says.

Mina looks at him with wide eyes, meeting his gaze for the first time. She shakes her head and her lips tremble.

"No," she says, her voice barely above a whisper. "Oh, no."

Her fear is palpable, rolling off her in waves. It makes me feel sorry for her. When I see tears welling up in her eyes, it's more than I can stand. I rush over and embrace her. She stiffens, but I continue to hold her. It isn't long before she relaxes, and the tears are flowing down her face.

"What is it?" I ask.

"You don't say no," she says. "It doesn't happen. No, you can't say no, no."

She's shaking her head violently, emphasizing each time she says the word no.

"It's okay," I say. "We'll be at dinner. What time should we be there?"

"One hour," she says.

She pulls herself out of my embrace and wipes at her tears. She nods and then turns walking away without another word. Efram and I look at each other, and I just shake my head. There are no words.

I pick up the dress and hold it up. It's nice, and not nearly what I was afraid it would be. I had half-assumed it would be some kind of a slutty show-off piece. The fact that it's not brings its own form of relief. The dress is a nice teal and it's covered with sequins but doesn't leave anything exposed that shouldn't be. Resigning myself, I go to dress for dinner.

WHEN WE WALK INTO THE DINING AREA, IT HAS BEEN transformed into a sad attempt at a royal dinner. Various pieces of cloth are draped around the walls in a mishmash of colors that don't go together. The tables are lined up into two long rows leading the way up towards a single large table that has been set on top of a stack of pallets.

The people of Wormwood Bunker are dressed in a mishmash as well. While at first glance they appear to be well-dressed, closer inspection reveals the flaws. Everything they have on is worn and has been patched multiple times. I noticed when I was putting on the dress that was sent to me that it was very threadbare. I assumed it was because they were stretching, and I was not a citizen, but being here tells a different story. They're barely surviving.

Hunter sits at the front table with two women on either side of him. He rises to his feet as we enter, clapping his hands. Silence falls across the room. All eyes turn to us. Great, it's not like I was already uncomfortable or anything, let's add to it. Probably because he senses my hesitation, Efram takes my hand in his and squeezes reassuringly. I give him a smile.

"Our guests of honor have arrived," Hunter says. "Please, make them feel welcome!"

Everyone stands and applauds like we're some kind of returning heroes. My cheeks burn, and I stare at the floor in front of us. Shifting from foot to foot, I wait for it to be over. I don't want to be here. My magic rises, tingling across my skin, and I know I have at least one way out. Not a good one. Efram must sense it because he tightens his grip on my hand.

"Careful," he hisses.

Yeah, right. It doesn't matter that they're all crazy—I can't create a scene here.

"Come," Hunter says, motioning us forward. "Join me. We're having a feast in your honor."

In our honor? Due to what? Because we showed up? This

is the craziest thing ever. Another testament to how insane this place is.

Be that as it may, Efram and I walk between the rows of tables and around to the seats on Hunter's right. He resumes his seat, and once he does, everyone else sits down. The clatter of silverware and chairs echoes.

Hunter picks up a small bell sitting next to his plate. He listens carefully then shakes it. A crystal-clear ringing sound echoes. Servants carrying trays laden with food march out. The first course is quickly placed before each of the guests. I stare at it and realize I have no idea what it is. It smells good, edible at least, but knowing what we found earlier I'm scared to try it.

Efram passes his hand over it casually, and I feel his magic surge. He mouths to me that it's okay. I nod and then go ahead and eat whatever the hell it is on my plate. There's a little buzz of conversation around the room, but it never grows very loud.

"So, what brought you to our Bunker? All of us have a tale of how we ended up here," Hunter asks, after the second course is served. "We want to hear your story."

My hand stops halfway to my mouth with a forkful of food. I swallow the last of what's in my mouth, glance at Efram, and then smile at Hunter.

"I'm sure it's not that interesting," I reply.

"No," Hunter says, idiotic grinning turning fully on me. "We want to hear it, don't we?"

He motions out across the room, and there's an immediate response of people murmuring and nodding. If they're actually interested or just afraid of and weirded out by Hunter I can't tell. All their eyes are on us, and it's clear we're not going to get out of this without telling some kind of a story. Efram clears his throat, and I think he's about to say something, but I jump into the pool with both feet.

"We were traveling when our railcar was attacked," I say, using part of the truth to give more meat to the lie and avoid telling too much. "We're supposed to be at Bunker 3 but of course, we didn't make it. We're so glad you took us in. If you hadn't..."

I trail off and stare into the distance, even summoning a tear to help sell the story.

"We lost several of our companions," Efram adds, embellishing the story.

"A sad tale," Hunter says, nodding enthusiastically. "What happened to them?"

He leans towards me in a manner that is somehow even creepier. His energy is so wrong. It's bad enough being in the same room with him, but when he comes closer it's worse. My skin crawls, and every fiber of me wants to run away from him. Anything to escape his presence. Bile rises in my throat, and I have to force it down. Throwing up on your host is probably bad form, not that I'm ever going to win any awards for my social skills.

"Dead," I say, forcing my voice neutral.

He waits, leaning in closer, it feels like he's begging for more without saying a word. He wants the details, and I don't want to give them and not just because I'm making this up. I don't want to do anything that makes him happy. He's too damn creepy.

"Well..." he says, trailing off himself raising the sensation of tension between us.

If nothing else, I can be one stubborn bitch when I want to and right now I want nothing more. Mentally I dig in my heels, making up my mind that there's no way in all the nine hells I'm going to play along with whatever his sick game is. Screw you, Hunter.

"It's too gruesome to relate," Efram says. I squeeze his thigh under the table digging my nails in making sure he knows I want him to shut up. "This dinner is too nice to sully with it."

"Right," Hunter says, the tension drains as he leans back in his seat. "Dinner."

He looks around. Everyone is staring at him waiting, I could hear a pin drop in the back of the room. My skin itches and crawls as my magic rises in anticipation. Everything about this situation is wrong. It's not just his creep factor, which is off the charts, it's the way everybody acts. The way they look at him. It's like they're afraid to breathe without his permission. I don't know what he is, and that worries me.

"What are you waiting for?" Hunter exclaims suddenly. "Bring on the next course!"

Now everything returns to some semblance of normal. Everyone starts eating and the slow buzz of conversation resumes. The servants come out, clearing the plates in front of us away and replacing them with a fresh course.

I stare at the... thing on my plate. I'm not sure what it is but it looks disgusting. I'm relatively sure it's meat but I have no idea what the source is. If I had to hazard a guess it looks like it's a sausage? Maybe? Oh God, please let it be a sausage. My stomach turns as I consider the other possibility of what might be and where it might've come from.

Meat is hard to come by in the Apocalypse. Domestic animals were one of the first casualties. Between people over farming them and the general difficulty of trying to raise them underground in limited space it's a luxury reserved for the rich. Out of the corner of my eye I notice Efram passing his hand over the plate, casually. He recoils, slightly, doing his best to cover it up, but I don't miss it. I catch his eye, and he gives me the barest of head shakes. Thanks, as if I needed any more encouragement to not eat whatever the hell it is on my plate.

"You absolutely must try the meat," Hunter says, staring at

the two of us with his fixed smile and crazy eyes. "It's to die for."

Great choice of words there, Hunter. Since that's exactly what I'm afraid will happen. Now that I think of it, that could be the best thing that could happen. It's the Apocalypse, there are worse things than dying.

"We rarely eat meat," Efram says. "It really doesn't agree with us."

"But I insist," Hunter says, his voice soft and menacing.

The room drops into silence once more. Efram and Hunter stare at each other, a contest of wills.

"And we both really appreciate it," Efram says. "I'm sure though that you do not wish to make your guests ill. The last time we had meat our bodies rejected it. It was highly unpleasant."

"I see," Hunter says, nodding slowly.

He continues staring but Efram meets his gaze apparently unfazed. A slow smile spreads across Efram's face, and I feel his energy shifting. My own magic rises, and I glance around the room noting the exits and the positioning of everyone else. To say we're outnumbered would be an understatement, but at the same time I feel confident we can get out of here if we need to.

I can't get a read on Hunter. That's part of what I find to be so wrong with him. I instinctively read the energy of everyone I meet, and it tells me a lot. I don't get that same feedback when I look at Hunter. He's hiding his true nature.

"I hope you understand," Efram continues. "We don't want to be rude, but I believe it would be more insulting if we were to be such poor company as to allow ourselves to become sick."

The tension builds. The hair on my arms stands on end. This is going to go bad, I can feel it. My breath becomes shallow and my heart rate increases. Hunter and Efram stare at each other in a battle of wills. Every eye in the room is on us. I slowly clench a fist, preparing.

"Of course," Hunter says, laughing.

I take my first deep breath and let it out. My heart rate slows to normal as the moment passes. Dammit, that was close. Hunter digs into his plate making a show of eating the meat. The strangeness of the situation continues to bother me, but it is what it is. We must get through it. I really wish Rafe and Nathaniel would get back. I'd love to be out of here.

Cordy walks forward to stand in front of Efram and me. He wrings his hands and looks from me over to Hunter then back to me.

"Hi Cordy," I say, trying to encourage him.

It seems to help, he straightens up and squares his shoulders. His hands drop to his sides, and a small smile appears on his face. Out of the corner of my eye, I notice Hunter is watching us with interest, but he doesn't say anything.

"I just want to suggest that you all get a blood mark," Cordy says. "It'll keep the haunts out of your head. You need all the protection you can get from them."

I don't know what it is about the words he says, but a cold chill runs down my spine. A blood mark? It doesn't sound like something I'm interested in having. I think I'll stick to my sigils that Nathaniel has given me.

"Thank you," I say, not wanting to be mean. "We will take that under advisement."

Cordy nods enthusiastically, almost like he becomes a bobblehead. He backs away without turning around continuing to nod.

"You got to be careful," he says. "The haunts are getting more restless."

"We will," I say.

"I think we should retire for the night," Efram says,

directing his words towards Hunter. "This meal has been quite delightful. A true pleasure."

"I'm glad you enjoyed it," Hunter says, his face and eyes unreadable.

"It was truly an enlightening experience," Efram says, rising to his feet.

I stand up along with him. Everyone in the room has once again stopped and is watching the exchange between Hunter and me. It's strangely like being on a television show, being the center of attention whether you want it or not. Everyone waiting to see what happens next as if some great cliffhanger is about to be revealed.

I follow Efram around the table, and we make our way down between the rows of onlookers to exit the dining hall. Their eyes bore into me but I do my best to ignore it.

Breathe, Aviella, I remind myself. Keep your shoulders square, stand up straight, don't slouch, good. One foot in front of the other.

When we turn the corner, I breathe a sigh of relief. No longer having their eyes upon me is a huge weight off. Silently Efram and I make our way back to the room we've claimed as our bunks. Once we're in there Efram looks around making sure that we're alone. The only sounds are the low roars that have become the white noise of Wormwood. Screeches of monsters and roars of what Efram says are mammoths. It's run-of-the-mill.

"Thank God that's over," I say. "Where in the hell are Rafe and Nathaniel?"

"They'll be back soon," Efram says, a certainty in his voice.

"Are you sure?

Efram grimaces and avoids my direct gaze.

"They damn well better be," he mutters.

I feel like I need to take a shower, but I know it won't do

any good. What I want is to wash the feel of this place away. It's gross and pervasive and I don't like it. As if on cue there is a particularly raucous round of screeches and howls that make me jump. Efram wraps his arms around me, and I return the embrace gratefully.

"Thank you," I say, my voice muffled by his chest.

"For what?" he asks.

"For being you," I say, my heart swelling.

Our energy intertwines as I embrace him in a way that is more than physical. He holds me until the noise dies down and at last we both step apart, if somewhat reluctantly.

"You should get some sleep," he says.

"Yeah," I agree.

I am exhausted. A weariness ago that goes clear down into my bones. Dealing with Hunter is draining. I climb up into the bunk and pull a cover over. Efram sits down at the table and leans his chair back against the wall.

My eyes drift closed, and I'm just about asleep when the sound of buzzing outside the walls jerks me awake. It's definitely locusts, and it sounds like they're trying to eat their way through the metal walls. My heart pounds and I can't catch my breath.

"It's a swarm of them," Efram says, standing next to the bunk. "They'll pass soon, they can't get in here."

He takes my hands in his, and a relaxing warmth spreads up through my arms reaching into my chest. My heart rate slows, and I'm able to breathe normally again. Swallowing, I nod and lie back down. Efram stands watch over me as I drift off to sleep. Knowing he's there, I feel safe. Hopefully in the morning Rafe and Nathaniel will be back.

CHAPTER TWELVE

*E*fram and Rafe walk towards me. They're both grinning and their eyes are alight with delight. Then it suddenly hits me that I'm naked.

"Guys, what's happening," I say, trying to cover myself up.

I reach for a towel or blanket or something to cover myself, but I can't pick up anything. Hands refuse to clench. I look back at the two guys approaching and they laugh.

"It's okay, Aviella," Rafe says, but it's not his voice. Something's wrong.

"We just want to make you ours," he says.

"You belong with us," Efram says.

Their faces are changing. Something is way wrong. My heart pounds, and I reach for my magic. An empty void is where it should be. There's nothing. Fear grips me as cold sweat forms across my skin.

"No," I say, shaking my head from side to side.

Their hands reach for me, but it's not their hands. Reddish skin ending in black talons reaches, grasping at the air in front of me. I open my mouth to scream but no sound comes out. I try to back away but it's like I'm moving through heavy water. Their eyes glow with an infernal light. On their foreheads is that same symbol that has haunted my dreams.

"Aviella," their voice melts into one, hollow and echoing. "You belong to us."

I trip as I back up, falling and falling and then I slam down on the bed; my eyes jerk open as I startle awake. A loud moaning assaults my ears. Rolling onto my side, my skin tingles in response to active magic.

I blink rapidly trying to clear the sleep from my eyes. Is this real?

Ethereal apparitions pour into the room, coming through the walls. Efram is fighting against them, weaving spells, throwing up shields and trying to hold them at bay. The hair on my arms stands on end, electric with the magic in the air.

"Aviella, be careful," Efram yells over his shoulder.

I drop off my bunk and land on my feet, pulling my magic. Thankfully, it responds as it should. The things approaching us must be the haunts that Cordy warned us about. They are pale, almost see-through, with drawn faces floating through the air. I don't know what they can do to us, and I don't want to find out. The room is filled with their moans, which make my ears ache. It's heartbreaking. There's a pulsing emptiness, an overwhelming sadness to their situation.

While they're attacking Efram, the ones approaching me pause. They lean in but don't reach forward. I'm surrounded by the creatures, and all of them cock their heads looking at me.

"It's not safe, hide. It's not safe."

All of them speak as one, and the voice is hollow and terrifying.

"What you mean?" I ask.

"I mean, fight!" Efram says. "Are you okay?"

"Not you," I respond.

"Who the hell are you talking to?" Efram asks amidst a flash of light, as he throws a magic bolt through one of the creatures.

"It's not safe. Hide. Run!"

They stare, empty eyes focused on me, and there's a strange depth to them. Everything else drops away. I have to listen to them. They know something I need to know. They're warning me, but what are they warning me away from?

"Aviella!" Efram yells.

It seems like his voice comes from a long distance. Down the tunnel, drifting towards me. I should respond. Maybe not. It doesn't matter, I have to figure this out.

Are they playing with my head? Is this real?

They motion, shaking their heads, continuing to speak in a chorus of one unified voice. It's fascinating, pulling me in, holding my attention.

Aviella, a voice, different and distant. It sounds like it's coming across a really bad phone connection. Filled with static and crackling.

"Who is that?" I ask.

"Aviella, who are you talking to," Efram says, urgency in his voice. "Fight! Are you okay?"

"I'm fine," I snap. "Let me listen."

The haunts repeat the phrase over and over. I try to focus beyond it.

Aviella, wake up. You have to wake up now!

"Daddy?" My voice trembles. It can't be, can it?

Wake up! Sweet baby, you've got to wake up now!

"Daddy!"

It's him, I know it. It still sounds like he's talking to me from a tunnel filled with static and interference. I don't know what he is saying, it doesn't make any sense. Wake up, I did wake up!

"Aviella, who are you talking to? Come on girl, talk to me," Efram says, desperation in his voice.

"It's my dad," I say. "He says we have to wake up."

"What?" Efram asks, glancing over his shoulder at me.

It's a dream, Aviella. Wake up.

The haunts surrounding me yell at me that I should run and hide. I have to figure this out. Am I still sleep? There's only one way to know.

I slap myself across the face with everything I've got. My hand and cheek both sting then I jerk and sit up. Awake.

Panting heavily, I drop off the bunk and look around. Efram jumps to his feet from his chair across the room. He looks around quickly, magic rising.

There's motion over by the door, then the sound of padded feet running. A boy darts down the hall. It's the first child we've seen here. Efram bursts into a run chasing after the boy. The adrenaline drains out of my system, leaving me shaking. I drop to the bed behind me, sitting on the edge and focusing on breathing.

A boy. Was he sending the haunts? Why haven't we seen him before? He wasn't at the meal or around at any point. This place gets weirder all the time. Breathe, one breath after another.

Was that my dad? It sounded like him, but it was a dream, wasn't it? Or was that how these haunts attack? Pulling us into half-awake, half-dream state. If it was my dad that would confirm everything I've believed, he's alive. I like that, a lot.

Efram walks back in empty-handed, shoulders slumped.

"Lose him?" I ask.

"Yeah," Efram says, shaking his head.

"I haven't seen him around here before," I say. "Do you think he was the one sending the apparitions?"

"I don't know," Efram says, with a sigh that goes down to his toes.

He comes over and sits on the bed next to me. We sit in an uneasy silence. My thoughts are consumed by trying to figure out what happened. Why did they react differently to me? They were attacking Efram, but me they warned. How did my dad reach out to me? None of this makes sense. Sighing, I'm about to say something when I hear footsteps running down the hallway.

Efram and I both are on our feet in an instant. I weave a shield in front of myself just in case, and Efram does the same. There's no telling what kind of oddity will come running in here next. We have to be ready for anything.

Rafe runs into the room with Nathaniel close on his heels. Rafe skids to stop in front of me as Nathaniel slams the door shut and leans against it.

"We have to get out of here, now," Rafe says, chest heaving with exertion.

"Rafe!" I exclaim.

"It's about time," Efram says.

"Yeah, glad to see you guys, too," Rafe says. "Now start packing."

"What's happening?" I ask, trying to get a grasp on the situation.

Nathaniel strides over to stand next to Rafe. He crosses his arms over his chest and clears his throat.

"We ran into some of our contacts," Nathaniel says.

"My contacts," Rafe inserts.

Nathaniel glares, shaking his head.

"Rafe's contacts," he says, correcting himself. Rafe grins broadly. "Another trumpet is going to sound, soon."

"And we can't be here when it happens," Rafe says.

"Why would it be safer to be possibly caught outside?" Efram asks.

Rafe and Nathaniel look at each other once more and Nathaniel gives a slow nod.

"According to my contacts people here tend to disappear," Rafe says. "This is not a good place. Worse than we thought."

"You're telling me," I say.

"What happened," Nathaniel asks, stepping forward and placing a hand on my shoulder.

It's my turn to exchange a glance with Efram. He shrugs and nods, indicating I should tell the story. I fill Rafe and Nathaniel in on everything that's happened so far, including the weird dinner with Hunter and our concerns about the food. I hesitate when I get up to the part about the haunts and the attack that just happened.

Nathaniel's hand on my shoulder warms, and I feel him pushing strength into me through his magic and the connection between us. Focusing on that, I become aware that all three of them, in their own, individual ways are doing the same. Swallowing hard I bite the bullet.

"I think my dad reached out to me, somehow," I say, biting my lower lip.

"What do you mean," Nathaniel asks.

I shake my head, uncertain how to put it into words.

"The haunts weren't attacking me," I say. "At least not directly. They were warning me. Telling me I should run and hide. It was... mesmerizing. I was struggling against it when I heard my dad's voice. He told me to wake up. It was only by listening to him that I escaped the half-awake state where the haunts could attack."

Nathaniel frowns deeply and pulls back, even though he doesn't break the connection with my arm. Once more I'm certain the angel knows more than he's telling. I stare at his eyes, willing him to tell me the truth.

"That confirms it," Rafe says.

"Confirms what?" I ask.

"Your dad's alive," he says.

"How can you know that for sure?" Efram asks.

"I don't," Rafe says. "I believe in Aviella."

The three of them look at me, and my heart swells until I'm sure my chest will explode. I've never felt like I belong and certainly have never felt the way these guys make me feel. Their loyalty, trust, and their admiration are almost more than I know what to do with. It's overwhelming, and tears form in my eyes. A smile spreads across my face as I shake my head.

"I love you guys," I say.

No matter what happens, I know they have my back, and I have theirs.

"It's too late to leave now," Efram says, pushing past the emotions I can feel in all our energies.

"You're right. It's more dangerous to be outside than it is to stay here a bit longer," Nathaniel agrees.

"I'm not so sure about that," Rafe says. "But I'll go along with it."

"Since we're all in agreement," Efram continues, "I'll take first watch. You three should sleep."

No one argues, and we all head for our bunks.

CHAPTER THIRTEEN

"It's not going to be easy," Nathaniel says. "We need supplies."

I stretch and yawn. My sleep last night was fitful at best. Ever since I woke up, the three men have been debating the merits of various plans for getting out of here. They've yet to come to an agreement. I don't feel like I have anything to add, so I head out of the room to take one last look around.

Down one of the hallways I hear somebody whispering. It draws me forward out of curiosity, if nothing else. I pass by several rooms where people are working and doing various things, but none of them are the source of the sound that's pulling me ahead. After I turn a corner I find it at last.

Looking through a round window in a door I see Hunter standing in the middle of an empty room, alone. Well, mostly alone. He's whispering to haunts. I see their ethereal forms shifting around him. I can't see them clearly, but I know they're there. He continues whispering, but it doesn't make any sense to me. I can't make words out of what he's saying. Something touches my back and I jump, yelping.

"Sorry," Rafe says. "You wandered off, and I wanted to check on you."

Afraid I've given myself away, I look back through the window, but apparently Hunter is too consumed with what he's doing to have heard the sound. Trying to will my heart back into a normal pace, I walk away from the door before saying anything to Rafe. No need to risk drawing attention.

"You scared the devil out of me," I say.

Rafe grins even bigger as he arches an eyebrow. "And that's a bad thing?"

"You know what I mean," I snap.

"You're right," he says in an uncharacteristic display of humility. "I apologize."

"It's fine," I say, sighing. "My nerves are shot. Whatever the hell Hunter is, he's strange, and I don't like this place."

Rafe looks serious, a change in his overall demeanor.

"Hunter," he says, shaking his head. "No one aboveground knows what he is, nor do they suggest anyone attempt to find out. Apparently, he's been here for a very long time, and they say that he doesn't age."

I have that strange sensation like ants or bugs are crawling across my arms.

"Great," I say, swallowing hard. "Well nothing like a bit of mystery, huh?"

Rafe stands close, too close. It feels like his golden eyes are drinking me in. My heart rate increases in response to his closeness. His musky, male scent fills my nostrils. It's exciting and makes me feel a tightness deep in my core as desire rises. My mouth is dry, too dry to speak.

"I missed you," he says, voice soft and low.

My heart stops, and my skin feels feverish as my lips tremble. This is crazy, almost as crazy as Hunter. I nod, expressing my agreement, but we can't act on this now. It's stupid, the timing is all wrong, there's a million and one reasons, all of them legitimate. None of them matter. Almost involuntarily I lift onto my toes and close the distance between us. I'm drawn to him like gravity pulling me in. His deep, soulful eyes stare into mine. He doesn't lean in, but he doesn't pull back either. His lips part, inviting.

Something slams behind us. I jump, spinning around and landing in a partial crouch. Rafe's energy surges protectively around me. The hallway is empty, but again Hunter is slamming something else in the room. My stomach clenches tight, and goosebumps race across my arms.

"We need to move," Rafe whispers, taking the lead.

"Yeah," I agree, turning and following him.

The moment is broken, again. It was crazy anyway. I can't possibly let myself get carried away by any one of my protectors. How would it affect the rest of them if I did? The ramifications are too great to consider. No, I have to remain strong. Besides, I don't know what I want. My connection to each of them is strong and different. They each bring something unique to the table. How am I supposed to choose only one?

"You know it's hard, right?" Rafe asks.

"What is?" I ask, glancing over.

"You," he says, smiling.

"Huh?" I ask, shaking my head.

"We're all drawn to you," he says, shaking his head. "They all feel it, even if they won't admit it."

"Oh," I say, recoiling internally but trying to hide it.

"Don't worry, it will all work out," he says, confident as always.

"Yeah," I agree, half-hearted. "Hey, I'm going to the bathroom, I'll meet you back at the bunk."

He stops and turns towards me, shaking his head.

"I'm not sure that's a good idea," he says, looking back the way we came.

"I am *not* going to have a guardian while I use the restroom, Rafe. I can take care of myself," I say, digging my heels in.

He grits his teeth, his jaw tightening and brow furrowing. Finally, he nods his assent.

"Okay," he says, "but be careful. And hurry."

"I'm not going to make a career out of it," I snap.

He holds his hands up in surrender.

"I know, I know…" he stares down the hall. "I admit it, I'm worried. Okay?"

"Yeah," I agree, getting control of my emotions. "Sorry, I guess I'm on edge too."

He nods, and we part ways at the intersection, him heading to the bunk while I go towards the restroom. The restroom has four sinks with dirty, broken mirrors hanging over them, and four stalls behind them. I walk from one end to the other making sure I'm alone then go to the middle sink. I turn on the water which creaks then a slow trickle comes out. Splashing the cool water on my face, I take a deep breath and look at myself in the mirror.

"Get it together," I tell my wavering reflection.

Deep breaths, calm and cleansing. It's one of the tricks my Dad taught me. One I don't use enough. Splashing more water on my face, I finally feel refreshed and ready to face the guys again. I grab the door and pull. Nothing happens. Frowning, I pull harder, but this time I notice the rattle. It's locked!

"Do you think I don't hear the whispers?" Hunter says, right behind me.

I jump, magic rising as well as the hairs on back of my neck.

"I haven't given much thought to you at all," I lie, spinning on my heel to face him.

"Or maybe you think I'm afraid of your pet demon?" he

asks, staring at me with his fixed empty smile and crazy eyes. Cold chills run down my spine. "You all should be grateful for my hospitality."

He runs his fingers over my skin tracing the line of my jaw.

"You might do well to rethink that," I say, proud of the fact that my voice doesn't quaver.

"You skin glows like the moon," he says, his eyes taking on an eerie light of their own.

What *is* this asshole?

"Let me out of here," I say. "Or I'll scream."

His smile widens. "Go ahead, I dare you. Let's see what happens."

He takes his hand off my face holding it up between the two of us. His fingernails extend, growing longer and darker, until they are full-on talons. The shirt he is wearing is open far enough I see his shoulder and notice it looks like it has had a bite taken out of it. His face shimmers and for just an instant he looks like Rafe.

Holy Shit, he's a shape-shifter!

I've got to get out of here. The others have to know the truth. Waving my arms in front of me, I slam them together and create a blinding light out of my sigils like Nathaniel taught me. An obscuring mist fills the space around us, and I turn back towards the door, moving on memory. I fumble for the handle and pull, but once again nothing happens. Dammit, I have to get out of here.

I hear him moving behind me, forcing me away from the door. The problem with the obscuring mist is I can't see through it either.

"I can smell you," he says, and he giggles.

He giggles, what in the hell is this guy, a stereotype for every horror movie ever made? I'm stuck in a creepy game of cat and mouse. Moving away from him in the confined space of the restroom. We're tracking each other by sound alone. I back into the wall opposite of the door.

"Going to suck the marrow out of your bones," he whispers. "Your soul will be here to keep me company forever."

I bite my tongue, cutting off any witty retort I might've come up with. Feeling my way along I slide along the sinks, making my way back to the door. I'm holding out hope that it will open this time, not that I have any reason to think it will, but my magic is pulsing inside of me, and maybe I can figure out some way to use it to force the door.

"You're going to be mine," he whispers.

I'm almost to the door, I think, when it explodes open.

"GAHA OIAD NANAEEL OL OIAD," Nathaniel yells, bursting into the room.

As soon as he says the words I understand him. He's invoking the power of God. Hunter shrieks, a bloodcurdling scream. I let go of the mist that I've been holding onto to hide myself. As soon as it fades, I see Hunter cowering against the far wall. He's trying to protect his head with his arms and continues to scream as Nathaniel continues chanting. Rafe rushes in with a thick rope in his hands.

Hunter and Rafe struggle, but Nathaniel's chant has weakened Hunter, leaving him mostly powerless. In a few moments Rafe has him completely bound. If only for good measure, Rafe places a gag over his mouth. I walk over to Hunter and meet his crazy eyes.

"How about my pet demon now?" I ask. "Do you feel the fear?"

Hunter gnashes at the gag in his mouth, struggling against the ties. He can't break free though, Rafe has him under control. Rafe jerks him roughly upright holding him back from me.

"That's enough," Rafe says, his voice low and menacing.

"What are we going to do with him?" I ask.

"There's a place here in Wormwood where all hope is lost. We're going to put him there," Nathaniel says.

Hunter's eyes widen, and his mouth opens around the gag. He shakes his head "no" violently and struggles harder than ever against the rope binding him. A thrill of joy rises in me seeing his fear then suddenly he leaps forward. I stumble backwards tripping over something and falling onto my butt. Hunter hangs in the air over me for an instant and cold grips me. This is it, my own klutzy nature is going to be the end of me. Instinctively protecting my head with my arms, a yelp escapes me, and then he flies backwards.

"No, you don't!" Rafe yells.

Hunter lands in a heap on the floor in front of Rafe. Red hot rage rises, replacing the fear of a moment ago. I leap to my feet.

"You son-of-a-" I exclaim, closing on Hunter. I kick him in the ribs once, then twice. Nathaniel grabs me from behind, pinning my arms to my side. "Let me go!"

"Aviella, no," Nathaniel says. "This is not you."

That stops me. The anger is gone in an instant leaving cold emptiness behind. He's right, what am I doing? I relax in his grip.

"Right," I exhale.

Nathaniel loosens his grip, but his hands linger on my arms before he pulls them away. Warmth pulses on my skin reminding me of his touch as it moves into my core.

"He won't escape the place we're putting him," Rafe says, wrapping the rope holding Hunter's binding a few more times around his forearm to make sure he can't pull a stunt like that again.

"Good, he deserves nothing less," I say. "Hopefully the people of this Bunker will be relieved. Do you think the lost souls trapped here will be able to escape if he's gone?"

"Perhaps," Nathaniel says, shaking his head.

It's one of those moments where I feel like the angel knows more than he's saying but I know damn well he's not going to share.

"Wait at the bunk for us," Rafe says. "Efram is there."

I nod my agreement and leave them to it, walking back to the bunk. On my way I pass by the dining area, and when I do, Cordy voice is coming from inside.

"It's only a matter of time," Cordy says.

I look in the open door and see him standing on one of the tables. A handful of the other Bunker survivors look up at him.

"Soon a new monster will emerge, even if it is wearing human skin, and it will claim the twisted crown that rules this shadowy place," he says. "There's only one way to be safe. We must all have the blood mark."

He raises his right arm and pulls the sleeve down holding it out for them all to see. Blood runs down his arm from the deep cuts that are apparently self-inflicted. He's cut an occult symbol into his forearm. It's raw and infected, black at the edges where the flesh is rotting. Bile rises in my throat, and I think I might throw up. Closing my eyes, I rush past hurrying to the bunk.

CHAPTER FOURTEEN

"*A*re you sure that he's gone?" I ask. "This place needs a break. There's entirely too much crazy."

"There's no way he can escape there," Nathaniel says.

"Yeah, he's done for," Rafe says, casual as ever.

"It's one of those things, Aviella," Efram says. "There's only so much we can do or control. We have to keep our eye on the bigger picture."

I don't care that he's right, it pisses me off. I don't want him to be right. It doesn't matter how long we've been on the run, or how many times I've seen this happen. I want to make a difference in the world. I want to help these people.

"I know it sucks," Rafe says. I glare at the demon once more, wondering if he's reading my mind somehow. "The bigger picture is there, and that is your destiny. We all feel it. The greatest good is to keep you moving forward and keep you safe."

Nathaniel and Efram nod their agreement. Clenching my teeth, I shake my head, struggling to not fight with them just for the sake of fighting. It won't do any good, because they're right. As much as I hate it, their logic is sound.

"Fine," I agree, crossing my arms over my chest.

I'm being petulant, but I don't really care. It breaks my heart leaving these people here. I don't know where I would take them, or how I would make their lives better, but I feel like I should be able to.

"We need to move," Nathaniel says. "We have a journey ahead of us."

There's no arguing with that either.

"So, we're going to go outside?" I ask.

"Yes," Rafe says. "You and Efram will both need protective suits. There's a high radiation count out there."

"Great, sounds like a damn good time," I say. Rafe and Nathaniel exchange a look of worry. "Oh, come on, it can't be that bad, can it?"

"We should be ready for anything," Nathaniel says.

In a strange turn of events, Rafe nods agreement. The fact they never agree on anything, but they're in agreement on this makes my stomach clench. This is definitely going to be worse than I expected.

We don't waste time. Efram and I get into our protective suits and then we're making our way through the creepy tunnels. The corridors leading to the exit are winding and confusing. It isn't long before I'm completely lost. I'm certain that we're getting closer to the exit though, because the sounds of beasts are growing louder. We've been here long enough I'd almost grown used to it. Now it's making my skin crawl again. The roars are the least worrisome somehow. There's a low, moaning, keening sound that is worse. I don't know what creature is making it, but it makes me feel a cold emptiness.

We turn a corner, and there's a steel staircase rising to a heavy metal door with thick bars across it. It's obviously intended to keep something out. As bad as everything is inside here, I really don't want to meet whatever in the hell it is they were worried might get in.

"What's the worst that could happen?" Efram asks, obviously sensing my hesitation.

His easy smile and dancing eyes ease my tension. How can I be worried when I have these three great guys with me?

"You have nothing to fear Aviella," Nathaniel says.

"If anything comes after us, I'll throw Nathaniel at it," Rafe says, smiling his mischievous grin.

Nathaniel grimaces, but doesn't say anything. I can't help but laugh.

"Let me help you get that helmet on," Efram says.

We take a few moments to make sure Efram's and my suits are completely sealed. The entire thing would be pointless if we were to get poisoned by the very air outside. I focus on breathing and trying to keep my nerves calm. Efram grips my hand and nods, smiling. It's reassuring.

As we start climbing up the steps our feet clang loudly against the steel. It echoes off the tile walls, making me feel like were drumming out our own doom. Wow, there's a morbid thought for you. Pausing I take a deep breath, close my eyes, and focus. There is absolutely no reason for me to be so gloomy. I need to be in the moment and deal with whatever is in it with me.

Self-pep talk over I resume the climb. The stairs double back on themselves, going up three flights to the door above. When we reach the door, Nathaniel slides the bars aside. The sounds of beasts outside are louder, but that's to be expected. We're closer to where they are, after all.

When he pulls the door open, there's a loud scraping that turns to a screech right before the door jams only partway open. Nathaniel leans into it and forces the door the rest of the way. A murky light pours in through the opening. I can't see past the guys to the actual outside. Nathaniel walks out followed by Rafe. Efram looks at me, making sure I'm okay before he walks out himself. I give him a reassuring nod, feigning a confidence I don't feel. He smiles and walks out, then I follow.

I've been out and about in the Apocalypse enough that you'd think I would be prepared. I'm not, and this area is worse than most. It's literally like walking into hell. The land around us is not only blasted, it's black. The ground is rolling hills stretching for as far as I can see. Turning a slow circle, my stomach sinks. Nothing could possibly live here. There's not even a blade of grass.

Dotting the landscape are green pools of tepid water. The air is hot. I can feel it even inside the protective suit, like it's pushing through and trying to grab me. The sky has a green tint to its overcast gray. I guess I can count it as a win that I don't see any of the monsters I was constantly hearing down in the Bunker.

"We have to move," Nathaniel says, striding off without another word.

We fall in behind him and begin our journey. I hope that this is the worst we have to experience. I know Rafe is a demon, and maybe he can tell me that hell is worse, but this is the closest comparison to it I've ever experienced. I focus on breathing. Every time I get upset and breathe heavier it steams up the visor of my protective suit. If I stay calm and don't breathe too much it makes it easier to see. I can only imagine the scent of the air here. Down in the Bunkers the air had an acrid edge to it that I still taste in my mouth. I'm certain that it comes from out here.

We walk for what feels like at least an hour. It's hard to judge because the sun is hidden. I'm thirsty, so darn thirsty. Swallowing feels impossible. My mouth is dry as a desert and my eyes and throat hurt. My vision is blurry no matter how much I blink, and when I do it feels like I'm dragging sandpaper across my eyes. It's been a long time since I've had some water. I would desperately love to take this helmet off too. Sweat runs down my back and is matting my hair to my head. Surviving in the Apocalypse is so damn uncomfortable.

The ground rumbles beneath my feet. I look around for a source, but I don't see anything. Nathaniel stops ahead and looks around too. Efram moves protectively closer. The four of us look around trying to spot where the rumble is coming from, but nothing happens. My nerves start to ease, and my breathing returns to normal. Nathaniel looks worried but shakes his head and resumes walking.

A loud roar tears through the air. It's so deep it feels like my bones shake with it. Now I'm scared.

"Guys?" I ask, voice quavering.

Rafe turns towards me, and it looks like he's about to say something when the ground throws him into the air. He twists his body and lands in a three-point crouch. I'm knocked onto my butt, again. I bounce up into the air again and again. The ground is bucking beneath me. Efram crouches and grabs me, setting me back on my feet. I keep my knees bent and loose, so the ground doesn't throw me again.

Nathaniel holds his hand out to one side. Light flashes, and then a sword appears in his hand. His wings unfold in a flash, spreading wide as he takes on a silvery glow. Rafe steps up next to him, his eyes glowing golden, and he lowers into a defensive crouch. Looking in the direction they are, a monster comes into sight, cresting a hill.

It's huge. Bigger than a semi truck. It's scaled with tufts of hair around its neck. There are more tufts around it's fore and hind paws like a scraggly corona of thorns. It has a short, fleshy tail of inverted triangles pointing downward.

"Shit," Efram exclaims. "Mammoth!"

"That's a mammoth?" I ask, incredulous.

It opens its mouth and roars. I swear I'm almost knocked over by the force of the sound. It makes my body ache.

"Run," Efram says, pale, his eyes wide.

Nathaniel charges the beast. He looks like a tiny doll racing forward. The scale is so completely off. This thing is so massive it dominates the horizon. Rafe moves with Nathaniel, the two of them splitting to move in opposite directions.

Efram grabs my arm and pulls me back. I jerk my arm free of his grip.

"We have to help them," I shout.

"I have to protect you," he says, intent. "That's what they are doing, stay back from it."

"No, I can help," I protest.

"Look at that thing!" he shouts. "You can't, keep back and be ready to run if they get in trouble."

It's another one of those situations where I don't care that he's right. I want to be right. I'm powerful and I know it. I also know that if I get involved it will distract the boys. They'll be more worried about me than themselves. Swallowing my pride, I nod to Efram, agreeing to hang back.

So, as it turns out, fighting is a spectator sport. Nathaniel attacks the mammoth head-on, swinging his sword with quick movements that are almost too fast to follow. Rafe comes at it from the side, summoning a sword of his own.

Nathaniel leaps up holding himself in the air as he dodges the thing's head, which was trying to swallow him. Rafe stabs into it from the side, and it roars its pain. The blood from the wound is a thick green mucus.

Nathaniel drives in his sword, aiming for the thing's eye. The beast must instinctively realize this because it drops its head, and Nathaniel's sword scrapes harmlessly across the hard shell that encompasses the top of it. I'm proud of my guys. They work like a team. All their differences are set aside for the greater good. The fight goes back and forth. Suddenly the thing lifts its head and slams it to one side, catching Nathaniel by surprise. He tumbles through the air in a flurry of feathers.

"Nathaniel!" I scream, leaping forward.

Efram is quicker than I am, grabbing my arm and pulling me back.

"He'll be fine," he says.

I don't bother turning to argue. Nathaniel rights himself in the air, but the mammoth is closing with him. Rafe leaps up, landing on top of the creature. He runs down its back, light-footed and agile. When he reaches the thing's neck, he flips his sword up, spinning around, holding it double handed, he drives it down into the beast. The monster screams, and then drops to the ground, dead.

I let out a breath that I didn't realize I'd been holding.

"Oh, thank God," I exhale.

Rafe leaps from the top of the monster and lands lightly. Nathaniel drops to the ground and walks over to him. The two men stare at each other, and I feel the tension from here.

Surely, they can't continue this? Nathaniel nods and holds out a hand. Rafe stares at it for an instant and then takes it returning the nod. It's only a moment but it's a big change for the two of them. I smile, happy that my two men are finding common ground. The moment passes, and they return to Efram and me.

"Well that was fun," Rafe says, grinning.

"Your idea of fun is skewed," I say, shaking my head. "We should work on that."

"Your wish is my command," Rafe says, bowing and flourishing his arm.

I slap him, playfully. "You're awful."

"Me?" he asks, straightening and holding a hand to his chest with a smile that goes from ear to ear.

"If you are all quite finished," Nathaniel says, serious as always. "The danger out here has not lessened. If anything, it's more."

"More?" I ask.

"Yes," Nathaniel says, nodding. "That fight is quite likely to attract other... things."

"Oh," I say, my stomach sinking. "We should go then."

No one argues further or delays. We start walking, and the time goes by slowly. One foot in front of the other. The heat in my suit rising with each step until I'm sure going to die of thirst long before we reach our goal. Every step forward is harder. I want to take off the mask so bad. The feel of fresh air against my skin, and maybe even a cool breeze would be more welcome than I can put into words. I can't, and I know it, but damn it, if the urge doesn't grow worse with every passing moment.

Nathaniel must pick up on my distress, or it's because I'm slowing down. He drops back next to me and takes my hand. A burst of energy fills me, and it slakes the feeling of thirst. I look at him wide-eyed and thankful.

"It's a quick fix," he says, smiling. "We're almost there. You can do this."

"Thank you," I say, gratefully.

He nods and increases his pace, taking the lead once more. I follow along easier now, no longer feeling like I'm having to struggle for every step. We walk for what must be another two or three miles when I hear a loud buzzing sound. Knowing that nothing out here is safe I look around for the source.

Several hundred yards away, a dark cloud moves towards us. It's low to the ground and obviously the source of the sound.

"Uh, guys?" I ask.

"Dammit," Rafe says, stepping out of our line towards the coming cloud.

He waves his hands through the air, and magic moves under his touch. He weaves a spell that casts a shield across all of us.

"Stay close to each other," he says. "I don't know how hard this is going to be."

No one argues as we huddle together. The cloud moves towards us faster. My heart rate increases, and I'm breathing so hard the visor is fogging up. Efram takes one of my hands and Nathaniel grabs the other. They move forward, mostly ignoring the coming insects.

I'm not going to look. That's right, Aviella, just don't look. You don't need to see this. Ignore that sound. No, that's not stirring up those memories. That sound isn't anything like bugs hitting the windshield while dad was driving down the highway at high rates of speed when I was a kid. No, it can't be that. What's that? You heard a loud splat? No, you heard nothing. Don't look, don't look, don't look Aviella.

I look.

What can I say, I'm not very good at listening to myself either. Of course, as soon as I do, I wish I hadn't. I've seen the locust swarms, which are horrifying. Somehow, because somebody somewhere likes to screw with me, this is worse.

There are literally millions of them, possibly billions. Each insect is a giant dragonfly-like thing the size of my fist. They have scorpion-like tails and giant mandibles protrude from their open mouths, which are full of sharp teeth. I think the worst part is that their iridescent wings are actually pretty. They catch the dim light and reflect off tiny little rainbows from each one of them.

"Oh God," I say, stomach clenching tight and bile rising into my throat.

I'm not going to throw up. I'm not going to throw up. I'm in a suit, there's nowhere for it to go, I am not going to throw up.

For a nice change of pace, I listen to myself, and my stomach settles. I knew I shouldn't have looked. Ugh, so gross. I really hate the Apocalypse.

The insects crawl over the protective bubble that Rafe is maintaining around us, blocking off all view of the world at large. The light was dim before but now we're walking in virtual darkness surrounded by the buzz of demonic wings of doom. There's a gloomy thought.

"This sucks," I say.

"Tell me about it," Rafe says, gritting his teeth, sweat pouring down his brow.

"We need to do something," Efram observes.

"I've got an idea," Rafe says.

His eyes glow brightly then an aura flares to life around him with a hellish-red tint. He says something in a deep, booming voice that echoes through me, resonating. The shield around us flashes orange-red, and all the insects crawling on it are flash-fried with a zapping sound that is both sickening and thrilling at the same time. It's a giant bug zapper, welcome to redneck heaven on a large scale. Rafe looks over his shoulder, grinning.

"Nice!" I exclaim.

He bows, his eyes locking on mine.

"Your wish is my command," he says.

Efram snorts while Nathaniel frowns and strides past Rafe, hitting him with his shoulder as he does so. Rafe ignores Nathaniel.

"Thank you," I say.

Rafe keeps the new and improved shield up as we continue our journey. When any of the bugs come close, they're fried and either they figure this out or they grow bored because it isn't long before they're keeping a distance.

We travel on in silence. At some point I realize I'm no longer sweating and I'm feeling light-headed. I'm fairly certain that's a bad thing but there's nothing to be done about it. We have to get where we're going.

The land around us starts to change. It's slow and subtle at first so I miss it. Only when I look behind us do I notice. Blades of grass grows in patches to either side of the rugged path we're following then there is a twig of a tree with two green leaves. It's the first signs of life—well real, natural life, I've seen since we exited the Wormwood Bunker.

It brings hope, and with hope I find my second wind. My spirits lift as there are more and more patches of green. Life finds a way. Nature in all her glory is a beautiful thing. It refreshes my faith in a higher power, something that gives meaning to all of this.

No matter how much my mood improves, I'm still exhausted and dehydrated. Rafe looks around and smiles then lets the shield down. I glance quickly around myself and see that there is no sign of the bugs. That's a relief.

"We're almost there," Nathaniel says.

"Thank God," I observe.

The ground rises before us as we climb a hill. I don't think it would normally seem that bad but in my current physical condition it might as well be Mount Rainier. I finally have to stop and rest my hands on my legs while trying to catch my breath.

Nathaniel comes back to me. He crouches and grabs my hands, gripping them firmly. I feel energy flowing to me once more. It helps but not as much as the last time.

"We are close," Nathaniel says. "I promise, just over the hill."

I nod, unable to force words out of my dry throat and mouth. Nathaniel gives me a rare smile. Squeezing my hands one last time he rises and takes the lead. Pulling on depths of reserves I didn't know I had, I straighten and continue walking. Finally, at long last, I see the crest of the hill.

Almost there. Keep walking. I can do this. When we finally reach the top, I want to dance and wave my arms around. I don't have the energy for it, but the desire is there. The slope down the hill is not nearly as steep as it was to climb, and waiting at the bottom is Silas. He waves.

He's standing at a demarcation line. It's shockingly clear-cut almost as if some cosmic hand drew it. On our side, the mostly black and sick landscape, and across the line where he is, a lush, verdant version of heaven. I notice that Silas does not set foot across that line.

Screw it, I don't care how tired I am. I want out of this hellhole. Using gravity to my advantage, I break into a run. In moments I'm past Nathaniel, who exclaims as I run by. Following my example, the boys also break into a run. When I'm close enough, I leap across the line. Slamming down and dropping to my knees, I dramatically kiss the ground.

"And here I thought you'd be happy to see me," Silas says, laughing.

"You have no idea," I say. "Can I take this suit off yet?"

"Yes, it should be safe now," Silas answers.

I have the hood off before Nathaniel, Efram and Rafe arrive. Fresh, blessed air, on my skin and filling my lungs is the greatest relief I've ever had. Nothing could be so sweet. I'd be perfectly happy to collapse on the ground and lie here.

"Glad you made it," Efram says as he walks out. "How bad was it?"

"Nothing that I couldn't handle," Silas answers, an answer that doesn't answer anything, a skill that Silas is the master of. "I've arranged for us to be accepted into Bunker 3."

"Is it going to be safe there?" I ask.

Silas nods. "Yes, we will be fine there."

"It's not safe here," Nathaniel says. "We should not linger."

"I take it that's my key," Rafe says, and easy grin spreading across his face. "Pun intended."

He pulls his crossing key out of his pocket and waves it around, laughing at his own joke.

As if in response to Nathaniel's warning, there is a flutter of wings in the air. All of us look as one. A flock of birds is heading in our direction. They seem big, too big, and they seem to be heading straight for us. Definitely not normal avian behavior. Sometimes I swear my luck is absolutely the worst.

"Rafe, open the crossing," Silas says.

Nathaniel, Efram and Silas form a line in front of me. As the magic rises, the hair on my arms stand on end. Everybody is pulling on their power and the energies are electric. There's a buzz in the air, a thrill that runs through me. A small part of me watches these hunky men stepping forward, wanting to protect me, and I feel special. I feel like maybe I'm worth it somehow. It's a good feeling, and not one that I'm used to.

The flock of birds is close enough now for me to see their individual features. At one point in time they might've been buzzards. They have the bald, reddish heads I would associate with that, but their beaks have serrated edges that look razor-sharp. Their eyes have a slight greenish glow to them. They squawk as they come closer, a high-pitched screech that reminds me of nails on a chalkboard.

Nathaniel summons his sword and then Silas does the same. Okay I really need to learn that trick. I want a sword too. Efram weaves his fingers relying only on his magic. The first of the birds dives at them, and Nathaniel slices through it easily. A spray of goo flies through the air and some lands on my face. I yelp in surprise and disgust. All three of the men look over their shoulders as one to make sure I'm okay.

"Sorry," I say, wiping at the nastiness that's on my face.

They turn their attention back to the immediate problem. My magic rises, buzzing deep in my bones, and warming the air around me. There is a faint crackle of electricity as I focus it. I'm not sure what I'm going to do. I'm usually not when it comes to my powers, but I throw it forward with an intention to stop the birds.

The latest batch divebombs at the boys and then slams into something in midair as if they're hitting a wall. They splat and slide to the ground, their necks broken. I smile, knowing that somehow, even if it's not under my control, I did that.

"We need to go, now," Rafe yells. "I can't keep this door open for long."

Before I turn around I feel it sliding along my skin, something dark with an almost oily, greasy quality to it. When I do turn, the open gateway is completely different than what I've seen before. Instead of a tunnel of light this is a swirling mass of darkness shot through with streaks of red. My stomach sinks.

"We're going into that?" I ask.

"I didn't say it would be friendly," Rafe says, shaking his head.

"We don't have a choice," Nathaniel says.

Just because the Apocalypse loves to throw everything at me at once the ground rumbles. It's a familiar rumble now and we look at each other knowing damn well that a mammoth is coming.

"Oh hell," I say, shaking my head.

Steeling my resolve, I run into the open door.

CHAPTER FIFTEEN

I had assumed that the journey through this gate would be the same as my last. I was wrong. Instead of traveling down a long tunnel, albeit a dark one instead of light, I step out into a city square. It's dark, like night has fallen, but there's no signs of the Apocalypse. The buildings are not destroyed or decaying. No signs of the bombings. There's not even any monsters or screams of tortured souls or anything to indicate that we're in a hell realm.

Well-dressed people walk around going about their business. They all look like they're wearing their Sunday best. Dressed to the nines as if they've gone out for a show, putting themselves on display for all to see. Several of them glance at us, and I'm immediately self-conscious. I'm drenched in sweat and can't smell very good after all that has happened.

I turn a slow circle, my mouth agape, unsure what to make of this. A couple glance at me, shaking their heads. The man is obviously a demon—he has red skin and horns—but he's dressed in a gray tuxedo with a walking stick and even a monocle. The woman with him, who looks completely human, is wearing a dress that looks like it came out of an old Western. It's light blue, floor-length, with a cinched waist and a bustle in the back. She even has a bonnet on her head. They lean close to each other and whisper. They hurry away as if I'm the frightening one.

"Don't wear your disbelief on your face," Rafe says, stepping close. "Especially here. They'll use that."

I snap my mouth shut, taking his advice.

"It's just —," I stop, unable to find the words.

"I know," Rafe says, smiling. He places a comforting hand on my shoulder. "It's not what you expected. I got that. That doesn't make it any less dangerous. If anything, it's more dangerous."

I guess that makes sense. What's more dangerous? The devil in disguise, or the one who comes at you openly? I know I always prefer the one who comes at you openly. At least then you know where you stand.

"We should move quickly," Silas says.

"I agree," Rafe says. "I'm going to have to do some deals though."

"Is that wise?" Efram asks.

"It is what it is," Rafe says, uncharacteristically somber.

Nathaniel keeps to himself, obviously uncomfortable. His head is jerking from side to side as if he's trying to see everything at once. Knowing him, he probably is.

"How long will this take?" Nathaniel asks.

"I'll make it as quick as possible," Rafe answers. "In the meantime, we need to move this way."

We follow Rafe as he leads the way across the town square. The center of this area is a small open park. Trees, grass, and small benches dot the picturesque landscape. A sidewalk skirts around the outside of it, which Rafe keeps us on. I feel eyes on us more than I see them. Every time I try to catch people looking, they're not. It's as if they sense before I turn my head that I'm about to look. It doesn't lower my certainty that we're being watched and inspected; there are too many eyes on us.

When we leave the square, the crowds are thinner, and I breathe a sigh of relief. Rafe leads us quickly through the streets. I stare around in wonder, because I really can't believe this is what hell looks like. It's nothing like I would've expected. There are no flames, no pits, nothing to indicate Dante had a clue. It looks like any other city, before the Apocalypse anyway.

We walk for six city blocks before Rafe leads us around another corner. Small shops fill the buildings, and I stare wide-eyed. There's a café with sidewalk seating. Demonic creatures sit next to human-looking people sharing a meal. The sidewalk is crowded now, and Rafe weaves us through it expertly. The high pageantry appearance of everyone besides us makes our group stand out like a sore thumb. Rafe stops in front of a small shop and looks over his shoulder.

"Wait out here," he says, then walks inside.

Nathaniel stays glued to my side. It's obvious he's uncomfortable here. He's so close to me, I can't tell whether he or I attract the most attention. There's no denying we're the focal point of it though.

"What is Rafe doing?" I ask.

"He's striking a deal," Silas answers, staring through the dark window into the shop that Rafe entered.

"A deal?" I ask.

"Travel through this paradox is not free," Silas explains. "He's paying for access to the areas we need to pass through to reach the exit."

Silas eyes roam over me as he talks as if he's unwrapping me slowly, waiting for the perfect moment to stake his claim. A warm tingle rushes over my skin, and desire flashes white hot. The way he looks at me, I feel… sexy. Beautiful, desirable, all the things a girl wants to feel.

Nathaniel clears his throat as he bumps into me, breaking the spell of the moment. A shudder passes over me. My heart is racing, and I'm breathing heavy. Why does my life have to be so complicated? I could be happy with any one of these guys, but having to choose between all of them? That's not fair. How do I make such a choice? Each one of them is unique and special. More than that, each of them calls to a different part of me.

"We have to hurry up and get out of here," Nathaniel says.

"You think?" I ask, sarcastically.

"Yes," Nathaniel says, either oblivious or pointedly ignoring my sarcasm, which is rude in its own way.

"Why, thank you, Captain Obvious," I say, letting my irritation show.

"He's not wrong," Efram says, jumping into the fray. "We're attracting a lot of attention."

"I think we're all very much aware of that," Silas says.

Nathaniel and Efram turn to face Silas. The tension between the three of them is thick. Is it wrong of me that I find it kind of sexy? Three incredibly hot, beautiful men arguing over my attention, but I can't let this carry on.

"Guys," I say, moving so that I'm standing in the middle of them.

An image flashes through my head, and my cheeks burn red hot. There's an instant, just an instant, where I imagine myself at the center of their attention, but in a very, very different way.

"What did I miss?" Rafe asks, emerging from the store.

"Nothing," Silas answers.

"I see," Rafe says, his gaze going from one man to the next. Rafe's eyes dance with delight as a smile spreads across his face. "Well, gentlemen, I do believe there is more than enough of Aviella for all of us. There's no need for any dick-waving contests."

"RAFE!" I exclaim as the other three men's eyes widen, and they each look away.

"Yes, my love?" he asks, smiling even bigger.

"You're... you... ugh!" I must be as bright red as the demon I see sitting at the café across the street staring at us. I've never been more embarrassed.

"Of course," he says. "Now that that is out of the way, perhaps we can travel on?"

No one argues. Hell, none of us are looking at each other. I can't believe Rafe. Once again, I have to wonder if he's in my head, reading my thoughts, and if he is... I'm going to kill him. Read that one, Rafe.

Rafe takes my hand, pulling me into motion. He starts whistling as we walk down the sidewalk, him swinging our hands, and walking with his usual swagger. It takes me a few minutes to recognize the tune he's whistling but eventually I get it. He's whistling *Time Is on My Side*.

Jerk, I think as a smile spreads across my own face.

I can't stay mad at him, no matter, it seems, what he does. His natural esprit towards life is infectious. He lives in the moment, taking enjoyment from everything. I'm certain, underneath the façade, there is a deep pain and hurt, but he never lets that slow him down. It doesn't detract from the moment he's in or the joy he finds in those around him.

We walk along, doing our best to be inconspicuous, which is pretty much impossible. I hate feeling self-conscious. You think I'd be used to it, having been an outcast all my life, but it's the kind of thing you never get accustomed to. It's always uncomfortable. Here it's dangerous as well. I don't know how much longer we walk, when Rafe suddenly turns and pulls us down an alley. Once our group is gathered, he slides up along the wall and peeks around the corner. He watches the street we just left silently for several minutes. When he's satisfied, he turns and walks deeper into the alley. We follow him silently.

The alley is filled with trash and dirt. The back sides of the buildings are not nearly as nice as the front façades. Here there are signs of decay. Something runs off to the side, and I jump involuntarily before realizing it's a rat. Efram puts a hand on my shoulder to reassure me. None of us speak as we walk, being careful to not attract attention. Rafe comes to a steel door and stops. He knocks, and a peephole slides open. Two glowing red eyes look out.

"Asmodeus is an asshole," Rafe says.

I snort. The eyes looking through the slot glow brighter. There's a low, rumbling growl, then the sounds of locks being turned and a chain clinking. The door swings open. A huge man blocks the opening. His arms look as big as tree trunks, crossed over his massive, broad chest. He would look completely human if he didn't have two large tusks growing up from his bottom jaw curving into sharp points ending close to his nose.

"What you want, Rafe," the man-creature growls.

"What do we all want," Rafe asks, looking up and to his left, feigning a philosophic tone and stance. "The meaning of life? Find true love? Find a dentist who can help us with our overgrown tusks?"

"Ha ha, Rafe," the creature says. "I'll see you again in another couple of centuries."

The creature grabs the door and swings it shut, but Rafe stops it with his foot.

"Now, now, is that any way to treat an old friend, Frederick?" Rafe asks.

Nathaniel shifts from one foot to the other, drawing unintended attention to himself.

"What in the hell have you gotten into now, Rafe?" The

creature asks, staring at Nathaniel. "An angel? Seriously?"

"What can I say, I have friends in low places," Rafe responds, grinning.

"I don't want to know, and I don't want to be involved," Frederick says, pulling on the door.

"We need passage," Rafe says. "I'll pay."

"You will pay?" the creature asks, arching an eyebrow. I can hear the surprise in his voice and see it on his face. It makes me wonder how much this is going to cost.

"Yes," Rafe says.

Debate rages across the creature's face and behind his eyes. Finally, he nods and steps to one side, granting us entrance. Rafe leads the way and we follow. The creature closes the door behind us.

"You know the way," the creature says.

Rafe nods and leads the way down the long hallway. We pass several closed doors, behind which I think I hear sounds. What I hear, I don't want to. It has to be wrong, or maybe it's not. I am in hell after all. The sounds are disturbing and more in line with what I would expect of hell. No one else seems to notice, or at least they're not reacting.

We move fast until Rafe stops in front of a red door. He looks over his shoulder at our small group and smiles, but this time I see he's forcing it.

"Wait here," he says. "I have to buy our passage."

He doesn't wait before opening the door, slipping through, and closing it behind him.

"Can anybody tell me what's happening?" I ask.

"Nothing here is free," Silas says.

"That's not really an answer to the question. What's the price," I ask.

"He'll give up some of his energy. It will make him weaker for a while," Silas responds.

There's something about the way he says it that makes me

certain there's more. He didn't tell me all of it.

"And?" I ask, wanting to know the truth.

Silas shakes his head and grimaces. He rubs the bridge of his nose. I wait, silent, encouraging him to tell me everything.

"It's a dangerous thing," Silas says. "The one who takes his energy can use it."

"Use it for what?" I ask.

"A lot," Silas says, shaking his head. "Potentially it gives them power over Rafe."

"We have to stop him," I say.

The three men look at each other, then all of them shake their heads negative.

"He's made his choice," Silas says.

"There is no other way," Nathaniel says.

"Aviella, let him do this," Efram adds.

"We can't let him do this!" I say. "What is wrong with you guys? We stand up for each other. We can't let one of our own put himself in so much danger."

Anger pulses as I step towards the door and reach for the handle. Nathaniel moves in front of me, blocking the door, while Efram and Silas take hold of my arms on either side.

"Aviella," Silas says.

"No!" I yell. "This is not what we do. I can't lose him. I can't lose any of you guys."

Tears well in my eyes, threatening to fall. Memories of everything I've lost flood through me. Bunker E247 and all those lost souls. Rowan, the other innocents, and my Dad. His face floats through my memory, and I hear his voice, whispering, telling me I should be calm, be in control.

Damn it Dad, I think.

The door opens and Rafe walks out. He doesn't look any the worse for wear, maybe a little paler. He smiles, but this time it doesn't hit his eyes.

"Ready to go?" he asks.

Swallowing hard to get past the lump in my throat I nod, unable to speak. What's done is done, and there's nothing I can do to change it now. I resolve though, that I'm not going to keep letting others pay the price for me. They shouldn't have to sacrifice themselves. I'm not worth it.

We follow Rafe as he heads down the hall. It must be an optical illusion, but it seems like the hall gets longer as we go. I would swear it stretches before us as we walk. That can't be though, can it? Maybe it can, I don't know. It's weird, and makes my stomach queasy, kind of like going over hills too fast in a car.

Time seems to have no meaning in this place. I know it's passing, I can feel that, but there's nothing to measure it by. The only way to keep myself from feeling sick is to watch my feet. That way I bypass the sensations of the walls in the hallway stretching. It gives me some relief at least.

I'm staring at them so intently, I bump into Efram's back. When I look up we've stopped, and before us is a different kind of door. This one seems to be made of stone carved with ancient runes. Rafe passes a hand over them and they glow a fiery red as if they are on fire. That's not creepy, nope not at all.

There's a loud cracking sound like a giant stone breaking, and the door swings open. An acrid scent hits me in the face full force, and I gag. There's an instant where I think I hear screaming. It's not just any screaming, it sounds like somebody who's lost everything. It's only there for a moment, and then it's gone again. I would put it off to my imagination, but Nathaniel shudders.

Rafe turns towards me and pulls a dangling pendant out of a pocket. It's a gold chain with an amethyst stone on it. It swings back and forth catching what little light there is and reflecting it back. He holds it out towards me. When I look at the stone, inside it there is a swirling blackness that calls to me. It feels like a whirlpool, sucking me in and down, holding my attention. I rip myself away from it.

"You need to wear this," he says.

"Why?" I ask, arching an eyebrow.

"Protection," he says. "It will hide you from the worst of the hell realms. Once we're clear of them, you must discard it immediately."

"Because…" I trail off letting it hang in the air.

"Outside the hell realms, it can be used to track you by the same things it hides you from while inside the realms," he explains.

"Well isn't that a handy dichotomy," I quip. "Who is it that could trace me with it?'

"The dealer I got it from," Rafe says, shaking his head. "I don't trust him, but we don't have a choice right now."

Rafe's protective intention is clear, as well as the risks and price he's paid. I take the necklace and place it over my head. As the stone settles against my chest, a burst of energy pulses through me, causing cold chills to run down my spine.

"Oh!" I exclaim.

Rafe nods, but for perhaps the first time since I've known him, he's not smiling. I know this trip has cost him a lot, more than he'll probably ever tell me. I'm grateful to him. We needed to get out of Wormwood. I'm not sure how long it will take before the crazies there get out of my head.

"Here we go," Rafe says.

"Where is it we are going?" I ask.

"Travel down here is never in a straight line," Rafe explains. "We have to go down before we can get out."

"Oh," I say, not really understanding.

Rafe doesn't bother to explain more. He walks through the door and we follow.

CHAPTER SIXTEEN

We're in a new hallway but this one is lined with tall, fluted stone columns that rise into darkness. In between each of them, the shadows are thick and heavy. The hairs on the back of my neck stand on end, and I look around to see if somebody or something is watching us.

This hallway isn't stretching at least, so there's that. We move down it quickly and come to another door. Rafe passes his hand over it. More of those fiery runes light up and the door swings open.

We step out into a wet city street. A soft mist is falling. It's chilly, much colder than I'm used to. I shiver. It looks like we've emerged into the seedier part of hell. Neon lights stretch for as far as the eye can see in either direction. The crowd down here isn't one that's out for some grand pageantry, these are streetwise survivors.

No one seems to be paying attention to us. Our dress fits into this area much better than it did the previous one. Crowds of people move up and down the sidewalks, and loud music drifts out of several open doors. When I read what the neon lights are advertising, my stomach drops a little. Girls. Live, nude girls is the main message. So, we're in a red-light district, or hell's equivalent. Great.

"This way," Rafe says. Not waiting to see if we listen, he takes off.

Silas, Efram, and Nathaniel look at me. I shrug. What are we going to do? Hang out here? Sometimes the only way out is the way through. Rafe walks like he knows where he's going. I try not to think too much about that. How well does he know this place? Did he spend a lot of time here? Did he work here?

No, I'm not going to think about it. I don't want to know what Rafe has done in the past. He may be a demon, but now he's my friend. I'm not going to judge him for what he's had to do to survive. His actions now are all I'm going to take into consideration.

Scantily dressed women approach us as we walk. The guys do their best to ignore them, but some are pushier than others. One woman focuses her attention on me.

"Hey, little sister," she says. She's barely wearing any clothes, pieces of cloth strategically placed to hide the most important parts. "You look like you're down for a good time."

"No, thank you," I say, pointedly not meeting her eyes.

"What's the matter, don't you like what you see?" she asks, pulling aside the light jacket she wears to reveal enough flesh that she could be ready for a shower.

"It's not that," I say, stomach clenching tight and my nerves sending mixed signals throughout my body. "I'm not interested."

"I bet I could change your mind," she says.

"She said she's not interested," Nathaniel says, stepping between the two of us.

"Are you kidding me?" the woman exclaims. "What are you doing down here?"

"That's none of your business," Nathaniel says.

"Right," the woman says, walking away.

"That's not good," Rafe mutters under his breath. "We're almost where I want to be. We need to hurry."

As good as his word, he moves faster, grabbing my wrist and pulling me along. The others scramble to keep up as he maneuvers through the crowded street. He forces his way through the crowd by sheer force of will, and physically pushing when that fails.

The colorful people we're working our way through don't seem to mind. Now that we're away from where the girls were throwing themselves at us, no one seems to be paying us any special attention.

Rafe pauses to look around, but before I can ask where we're headed, he's pulling me along again. We come to a stop in front of an open door guarded by a huge, biker-looking guy. He has massive arms covered in tattoos. He's wearing a leather vest filled with patches, fingerless leather gloves, and jeans. There are tattoos and piercings on his face, and his head is shaved. He looks at Rafe with beady eyes.

"Hey, Tommy," Rafe says, smiling.

"Rafe," Tommy says.

"I need in," Rafe says.

"Sure," he answers, motioning towards the door.

"Thanks," Rafe says, sliding past Tommy.

Music pulses out of the open door. Following Rafe inside, we walk down a tight hallway, dimly lit. As we enter, the beat grows louder, pulsing against my chest. It's standard dance music, but something about it makes me want to swing my hips. Wouldn't it be nice to just let my hair down?

"I have to see somebody," Rafe says, shouting and leaning in close to be heard over the music. "This may take a little bit. You guys should relax. We should be safe here, I think."

I nod in answer. I don't feel like yelling to be heard over

the music. Rafe walks away leaving me alone with the other three men. Looking at Efram, I feel his desire. When I look at Silas, he looks as if he could devour me. Only Nathaniel seems stiff as ever.

"Let's dance," I say, smiling from ear to ear.

I walk backwards towards the dance floor, motioning with my hands that the boys should follow. Instinctively, I sway my hips from side to side as I go. The way the three of them look at me fills me with a burning desire. I want them.

They follow me, pulled in like planets caught in my gravity. The music is pounding, heavy dance beats of a repetitive nature, and I lose myself in it. In this moment, for this little while, I let myself forget everything. All the stress, all the pain, and all the loss are outside of this time. This moment, I'm dancing.

Silas moves in front of me placing his hands on my hips. Our bodies meld together as we dance. He leans in close enough that the rough stubble on his face scrapes my cheek. His arousal presses into my pelvis. Efram moves behind me placing his hands directly above Silas' and grinding against me from behind.

Nathaniel stands to one side, awkwardly, so I turn my attention towards him and smile. Holding out a hand, I beckon him to take it, pulling him in close. They form a triangle around me, and the four of us move in time with each other and the music. Their energies caress me like the touch of a sensual lover, as the pulsing music works its way into my soul. The deeper it drives, the further away it pushes all my worries.

There's nothing but us. Each of their energies is so unique I can close my eyes and identify them. It weaves in and out, entwining and separating. They rotate around me moving in and out. I feel one then another moving in close, pressing against me, taking turns. It's erotic and sensual and everything I've dreamed in my naughtiest fantasies. Maybe my dreams can come true.

I close my eyes and lean my head back, writhing with the music. Its sensual beats make my magic rise. Goosebumps run across my skin. I reach out and find Silas, stroking his energy. As I run my fingers down his face, a soft moan slips from my lips. My core is so tight, my lady bits are consuming my attention. There's an empty ache deep inside me wanting to be filled.

Running my hands through my hair, I sense Silas's pent-up desire. He barely contains it, it's consuming, and I'm tempted to throw myself into it.

Dancing back from that edge, I switch my attention to Efram. His energy is different. Protective, honorable, held back out of a sense of duty. I tease him, letting my energy caress him. His arousal pulses through it, feeding me. My senses are hyperaware.

When I reach for Nathaniel through our connection, his honor-bound stiffness is a wall between us. Much like Efram, he has a strong sense of duty and obligation. It doesn't matter. I sense his desire. He can try to hide it, but it won't work. It calls to me. He wants me as much as I want him.

On a whim, I try something different. Reaching out through my energy and magic, I embrace all three of the men at once. My mind explodes, expanding to take in a deeper and broader sense of awareness than I've had before. A shudder runs through me, almost interrupting my dance, but the music commands and I follow. There's no stopping the flow. I hear the boys gasp, or I sense it more than hear it.

Desire floods through me like a roaring whitewater river. I'm flooded with overwhelming feelings of love, devotion, and barely restrained passion. It's like nothing I've experienced. They want me. Any part of me they can have they'll take. And I, for my part, want to give myself to them completely. They are my men, mine.

Suddenly there's a hand on my shoulder, and I open my eyes as I'm jerked around to come face-to-face with Rafe.

"We have to get out of here, now," he says, urgency in his eyes and his voice.

"Rafe, what?" I exclaim.

When I open my eyes, it's obvious we're the center of attention. There's an empty circle in the middle of the dance floor occupied by the five of us. Everyone is watching. Rafe grabs my hand without a word, turning and pulling, but four burly men step out of the crowd, blocking the exit.

"Shit," Rafe says.

The biggest of the men shimmers, revealing blackened skin with glowing red cracks and horns. His eyes are empty pits where flames burn.

"Just hand over the girl," the demon says.

"That's not going to happen," Rafe tells them, eyes flaming red with thinly bridled rage.

"Whoa, buddy. She's got a price on her head. I'm not going to hurt her, I'm just cashing in. You know how it is down here," the demon says.

"I also know the price of ice water," Rafe answers. "You better bring a bigger army if you want to take her from us."

"Have it your way," the demon says.

Chaos erupts around us. Attacks come in from all sides. My heart pounds as I duck grasping arms. Quickly I weave my arms and slam my sigils together creating an obscuring mist. Hands grab my arms and I yelp, struggling against them.

"Aviella," Efram says. "Come with us."

Only then do I realize Silas and he have a hold of me.

Ducking, they pull us through the mist, dodging our attackers.

"Where's Rafe?" I ask.

"He can take care of himself," Silas says.

Looking over my shoulder, I can't see him. The mist and the bodies block my view. He has to be okay.

CHAPTER SEVENTEEN

RAFE

"*Y*ou should have known better than to go against me," I say, summoning my soul sword.

Energy swirls and coalesces around my hand as the blade forms. Red flames erupt, licking up and down the length of it. The demons circling me pause when they see it, and a smile comes unbidden to my lips.

My blood sings to the tune of the powers I'm channeling. It feels good to let go. No reason to hold back—it's not like I can kill them. I'll put them all down, but they'll be back up in an hour. Welcome to hell, there's nowhere else for them to go.

The best part though, it will hurt. A lot. They deserve that and so much more. The glee of it fills me, threatening to overwhelm, but I push it down. I can't give in to that. I'll lose myself in it if I do. Aviella needs me. Stay focused; stay in control.

"Dammit Rafe," the big one says, "we're just trying to get by. You of all people should understand this."

"You chose wrong," I growl. "That girl is under my protection."

"Then you've got lot bigger problems," he says. "Get him, boys, he can't take all of us."

They attack. Everything becomes motion as I give myself over to the flow of battle. I love the fluidity of it. Step, then move to the next position, sword slicing through the air and bodies the same. Burning wounds left in its path.

A fist connects with my head, jarring me. Stars dance in my vision, but I don't let it slow me down. In battle, there is no time for thought. Muscle memory takes over. Pain means nothing. The only thing that matters is moving to the next position, which my body does of its own accord. It's a dance, a sensual, loving dance between myself and my sword.

The sword crackles and whistles as it moves through the air. It combines with the shouts and screams, becoming a symphony of destruction. I am a Maestro, directing the orchestral movement until at last I stand alone.

I hold the sword two handed across my body, knees bent, looking around for my next attacker. My heart slows, and I take a deep breath, realizing they're all down. Lowering the sword, I don't dismiss it yet. I walk over to the leader of the crew, and crouch next to him. The open wound across his gut was cauterized as I sliced through, but I know from experience how badly it hurts. He looks up, whimpering, expecting more pain to come.

"You need to stay away from this one," I say. "She's mine."

"Rafe," he gasps, sweat pouring down his face. "You've got bigger problems, man. She's marked."

"I know," I say. "I'll deal with it."

I rise to my feet and step around the piles of bodies. The bartender is staring at me.

"Sorry about the mess," I say.

The bartender shrugs and resumes cleaning a glass. Chuckling, I walk out the door.

Outside, I reach out, stretching my awareness until I feel her. I let my sword dissipate before I draw too much attention and break into a jog. We need to get out of the hell realms before anything else happens. There are more rumors down here, believable ones, that a trumpet is about to sound. We can't be here when that happens.

Following my sense of her, I make my way through the crowded streets. There doesn't seem to be any commotion which is good. I'm not sure how far the word has spread about the bounty on her head, but no matter. It's best we get the hell out of here now, literally.

Silas must've listened well when I told him where to go to if we get in trouble. It seems he's following my directions exactly. Good, they'll be waiting at the next gate. Patting my pocket, I reassure myself that the key I just traded for is there. It would be one heck of a problem if I lost it in that scuffle back there.

When I turn the corner, I escape most of the crowds. This is a quiet side street without any bars. It's made up of mostly abandoned buildings. Double checking to make sure I'm not being followed, I make my way to a small house. It has a broken-down chain-link fence and overgrown yard. An unassuming clapboard structure with boarded-up windows. Only those of us in the know realize what's inside.

I approach the door carefully, not wanting to be assaulted the moment I poke my head through. Stopping outside, I make one last check of the street for any observing eyes before knocking.

"Friendly face here," I say, as I pull the door open. Nathaniel lowers his sword as I walk in, much as I expected.

"Were you able to get a key?" Silas asks.

Aviella stands next to him, and I sense her fear. Her wide eyes dart around nervously. She's terrified. A sharp pain stabs through my chest. I wish I hadn't brought her here. We didn't have a choice though.

"Yeah," I say. "We should get out of here."

No one argues. I lead the way through the small two-bedroom house into the kitchen. Dirty linoleum and rotting cabinets fill the air with a nasty, dirty smell. I pull the key out of my pocket and activate it. The portal opens with a whoosh. I usher the others through, stepping in myself just before it closes.

It's hard, sometimes, to remember that Aviella is new to this world. She's strong, so strong that I tend to not think about the effect of it on her. It's not fair, but then in my experience, nothing in this world is. I guess it would be better if we had any clue what the darkness wants with her. It would help all of us, since she's tied to us and into a bigger destiny. What that destiny is I have no idea. Not knowing is enough to scare me.

Silas leads the way through the portal tunnel. When we reached the far gate and step through we emerge into an abandoned mine shaft. Silas takes a moment to get his bearings and then leads the way. It's clear nothing has traveled this way for a very long time by the amount of dirt undisturbed, if nothing else.

"Bunker 3 should be just ahead," Silas says. "We'll be there shortly."

"Good," Efram says. His eyes shift quickly to Aviella, then away. "I'm glad we're out of the hell realms."

Aviella glances over her shoulder at him with an unreadable look. Did something happen back there that I don't know about? There's something about that look that I can't quite put my finger on.

Almost I could be jealous, but I'm not. I don't own her, and I don't want to. My feelings for her go too deep. If I were to try to own her, it would be like caging a wild bird and then wondering why it quit singing. Her beauty is in who she is; I have no desire to change it. I'm not sure the others can come to terms with that though. Which makes a problem. I don't want them to own her either.

We walk in an uneasy silence. I come up with different ideas about how to ease it but toss them aside as fast as they come. Nothing seems quite right. I'm consumed with figuring this out when I bump into Aviella. She's staring at the wall. I look at where she's looking. Strange symbols are carved into the walls of the tunnel. She stands before them transfixed. Silas steps up beside her on the other side.

"Some of these were in my vision," she says.

I try to read the energy around them, but it strains my abilities. No matter how I try to focus I can't seem to bring them into clarity. It's like when you're looking at something blurry and you try to will your eyes to make it clear, but it doesn't work. Anger flashes white hot in an instant, and I clench my fists.

No, I'm not going to let this get to me. I recognize it for what it is, my desire to make everything right for her. I can't let that control me or use it as an excuse for my emotions to run free.

"I do not recognize these," Silas says, making me feel slightly better. At least I'm not the only one.

We need solid answers. The symbols keep coming up and there has to be a reason. I can't help feeling they are the key to keeping her safe. Staring at them I come to a conclusion. Once she's safely tucked away inside Bunker 3, I'm going to find out what these mean. She'll be safe with the others, so I will go and figure it out. I don't care whose ass I have to beat to get the truth, someone knows it. I'm the best man for the job. No one else can travel where I do.

Certainty comes with my decision. I know it's the right move.

"We're almost there," Silas says. "We should hurry up."

Aviella tears her eyes away from the symbols and follows Silas. The way it holds onto her strengthens my resolve. I'm going to find out, for her. Everything for her.

CHAPTER EIGHTEEN

"*I*t's not much further," Silas says.

"Good," I answer, my stomach grumbling loudly. "I'm starving."

No one says anything. We're all hungry. It's been a long time since we last ate, apparently food isn't a thing in the hell realms. Does that mean Rafe doesn't need to eat? That doesn't make sense. I've seen him eat. Well maybe he eats just for show? Didn't Brad Pitt talk about that in that vampire movie he did? I have a dim memory of it playing on a hotel television while I was curled up next to my dad trying to sleep.

What a weird thing that would be, not having to eat. I'd take it right now though. God, I'm hungry. My stomach rumbles again, and my mouth decides to randomly water. Sorry, I got nothing for you to use all that saliva on.

The symbols keep floating across my thoughts, making the hunger an almost-welcome distraction. They mean something. I can almost grasp it, but every time I do, it slides away from me. It's that name hanging on the tip of your tongue, or the lyrics to a song you can't quite remember so you hum along with a nuh-nuh-nuh instead of the actual words.

Damn, it's annoying.

I can't help feeling that if I could figure this out, it would somehow save us. The world needs saving. All this misery and pain hurts me. Maybe I'm crazy, but I have this certainty that I can make a difference.

Truth is, I've probably gone insane. Who am I to be the Savior of the world? An orphan with delusions of grandeur? So what if I have some powers? Apparently in the Apocalypse lots of people do. It hasn't made any difference yet. I've barely been able to keep myself and my friends alive much less save anyone else. It all feels kind of pointless. Why survive when you can't do anything to make the world better?

Damn, my thoughts are going dark. Maybe it's the hunger. Shaking myself, I try to push away the morbidity. It's not easy because floating behind it are the symbols, flashing through my thoughts, and then I see that final image of Bunker E247. All those people lost. I couldn't save them.

"Hold," Nathaniel says, placing a hand in front of me.

"What is —," I say, then it hits.

The ground rumbles and dust falls from the ceiling. It increases in intensity until I'm knocked off my feet and land hard on my butt.

"We have to get out of this tunnel," Efram says.

I try to climb to my feet, but the ground is rocking so violently, I don't make it before I'm knocked back down again. Rafe scoops me into his arms and runs. Everyone groups, then we run in a small pack. The ground is shaking so violently now that rocks fall from the ceiling and cracks appear in the walls.

"Look out," Silas exclaims.

Rafe instinctively leaps to the left. He moves just as something crashes through where we were. My heart pounds and I shift my weight, forcing Rafe to put me down. He places an arm over my chest and tries to shield me protectively, but I'm having none of that. I can stand on my own.

In front of us, a fur-covered monstrosity rises from the rubble of the wall it burst through. It rises up onto its hind legs, turning towards us, growling, and revealing row after row of razor-sharp teeth. It's big, at least seven feet tall. It takes me more than a moment to figure out what it might be. My stomach turns when I figure out what I think it used to be a, mole. Now it's been twisted, either by government experiments or the nature of the Apocalypse. However it came to be, it's a formidable-looking opponent.

A sword appears in Rafe's right hand. Nathaniel summons his sword, and the two men step forward to attack the creature. It dodges their swings, swinging its own stocky arms that end in long black claws.

Nathaniel and Rafe dance backwards, avoiding the thing's swings. Efram shouts something in a language that seems dimly familiar. A glowing ball of light forms in his hands and he throws it at the creature. It strikes the thing upside the head and explodes, blinding me.

"Ah!" I cry out, stumbling backwards.

The creature screams too, but its scream sounds much more painful. I hear the sounds of sword slicing through flesh while I blink away the aftereffects of the blinding light. As my vision clears, I see the monster lying on the floor in a pool of its own blood.

"We have to move fast," Silas says.

As if in response, the tunnel bucks again, but this time I'm able to keep my footing. A long crack appears in the ceiling, letting dirt and gravel pour in. The tight quarters are filling with dust, making it hard to see. Breathing is becoming something you don't want to do.

Coughing, I run, somehow in the lead. A crack appears in the floor but it's small enough I leap across. Glancing over my shoulder I see the others make it, but it widens with each one coming over. Nathaniel's last, and by the time he reaches it, it's at least six feet across. I skid to a stop, fear creating cold chills down my arms.

"He's never going to make it," I say, gasping for air and coughing.

"He will," Rafe says, exuding confidence.

Nathaniel glances down at the wide opening as he leaps into the air. I'm certain that he's going to hit his head on the top of the tunnel, but he avoids that.

He's almost across.

My heart pounds so hard it might burst from my chest. His foot lands barely on the edge and I think he's made it but then another tremor rocks the ground.

He's thrown backwards. His arms pinwheel as he tries to remain upright.

"Nathaniel!" I scream.

He falls, horizontal to the floor. I rush towards him, but Rafe and Silas grab my arms, holding me back.

"I have to help him," I yell, struggling against their hold. They're too strong, I can't break free. "Dammit, let me go."

"Aviella, look," Rafe says.

I follow his gaze towards Nathaniel. The angel is outlined in silvery light, his wings fully exposed, lifting himself up out of the crack. He glides through the air and lands gracefully a couple of feet away.

Relief rushes through my veins, and tears well in my eyes. There's no time for a joyous reunion moment. The tunnel shakes once more, and now boulders are falling, mixed with the dirt and gravel. We turn and run, but the way ahead is almost blocked by a cave-in. Efram steps forward, chanting an incantation, and then he thrust his hands forward, palms out. Force reverberates down the tunnel, hits the rubble, and blasts it out of our way.

A bright light ahead—it's the end of the tunnel!

Staying close together and dodging falling debris, we rush. We're close, so close. Hope blossoms. We're going to make it!

The light comes closer, and I can feel the warmth of the sun touching my skin.

There's a deafening roar, then a tinny sound blasting that's not just heard, it's felt.

"The trumpet," Nathaniel says.

Nathaniel glows bright until he's outlined in blinding white light. Tingles run through my nervous system, the hair on my arm stands on end, and then my body stiffens, and my limbs stick straight out. I throw my head back and scream.

Power surges through me. It rises from the ground, burning through me. New pathways are opening in my mind. I can't process it.

It hurts so bad and there's no escape. I look ahead, staring into nothingness, then suddenly I see the symbols again. They float in front of my eyes, three dimensional images twisting and turning. Behind them, I see dimensions crashing one into another. Everything is changing.

Screams fill my head. I'm sure it's not me. Something is happening. People are dying. A demonic army riding horses and carrying flaming swords rides across my vision, cutting their way through everything. There is no escape.

I don't know what's real and what's not.

It's too much to deal with. I'm shaking, legs and arms weak.

I see a desert, and the pyramids are in the background. Rising out of the river, wings spread wide, are four angels, but they're giants. Ten feet tall at least. They're dressed in red robes, and their eyes blaze with a burning white light.

When they open their mouths, fire, smoke, and plagues pour out. The earth itself is crying out in pain and agony. My heart breaks, the pain in my chest so great I think it might kill me.

One of the red angels waves an arm and the demonic army of horsemen charges, riding across the land. I see them heading for a Bunker, and it's a massive one.

"No!" I cry out. "We have to save them!"

"Save who?" Efram asks.

"We can't," Nathaniel says.

Tears stream down my face as I watch the army of demons cut through the Bunker leaving no one alive.

"Grab her up," Silas orders. "We have to get out of this tunnel, now."

I'm lifted off my feet by strong arms, but I can't see who. The vision consumes all my attention. Suddenly everything is dark.

I'm thrown about, tossing like a ragdoll, shaking and weak. Gasping in air, I throw my arms around whoever is holding me and sob.

I wasn't fast enough. I should've been able to save them. It's all on me. I have to be better, we have to bring them hope, we have to save them.

The vision passes, and I regain a semblance of self-control, wiping away the tears. When I can see at last, it's Efram carrying me.

"I'm good," I say, a final sob racking my body.

"Are you sure?" he asks, his concern thick and heavy, like a warm blanket covering me.

I nod, not trusting my voice. He stares into my eyes before setting me on my feet. I let my fingers linger on his cheek, feeling the several days' growth. It's kind of nice, and it strengthens his jawline, in a way it makes him even sexier. We step out of the tunnel, but the sky is dark.

"What happened to the sun?" I ask.

"The trumpet," Nathaniel answers.

There's nothing more to be said about that. I look around. We're in a mountainous region, Colorado maybe. We've come into an open area surrounded on all sides by the rising peaks of the mountains. The center is dominated by a huge lake that stretches out as far as I can see in the dim light.

In the center of the lake is an island with a massive structure on it. The structure has seen better days but is still standing. Silas is standing ahead, close to the lake, and staring out at the island.

"Is that Bunker 3?" I ask.

"Yes," Efram says.

"Huh, look at that," Rafe comments, pointing at the ground.

There are hoof prints. Hundreds, maybe thousands or more of them. The army I saw in my vision? Here? No... it couldn't be, could it? Nathaniel stands off to one side, stoic as ever, and apparently doing his best to ignore the rest of us. I don't envy him his position. I know, with a deep certainty, that he knows things he can't tell us. I also understand it's not that he doesn't want to, but because of his very nature. He can't go against it; he can't betray the trust pinning him to heaven. It sucks. If we knew what he knew, our lives would probably be much easier. Or not. Maybe they'd just be worse.

"Damn," Silas says. "We need to get into the Bunker."

"How?" I ask, looking at the lake between us and it.

The lake is beautiful, reflecting the mountains and sky. I don't know why, but I don't like it. There's something about it that makes me pull back. It looks so smooth and perfect, like some giant laid a mirror down in this clearing. Is that what it is?

"There's a boat there," Efram says.

Helpful, Efram, thanks. Great. When I look at where he's

pointing, I wouldn't call what he's indicating a boat. A raft, maybe. A crappy, falling-apart raft at that. It definitely doesn't look safe or like anything I want to be riding across a lake that is who knows how deep.

"Yeah…" I say, trailing off.

"What's wrong, Aviella?" Rafe asks, picking up on my discomfort.

"Nothing, just… I…" I try to say it, but I can't.

My cheeks burn hot, and my skin is cold and clammy. They're all looking at me, and I want to crawl under a rock I'm so embarrassed.

"Aviella, it will be fine," Nathaniel says.

"I can't swim!" it bursts out.

They look at each other, then back at me.

"That's okay. We're going to be in a boat," Efram says.

"That's not a boat! It's a wreck," I say, pointing at the thing.

"I assure you, it will get us where we are going," Silas says.

"Right," I say, shaking my head. "How about I stay out here, and you guys go ahead? I'll follow, okay?"

I wish I was kidding, but I'm not. The way that boat looks terrifies me. I know I'm being irrational, but it doesn't matter. I can't do that. No way, no how.

"Aviella," Nathaniel says. Taking my hands in his, he stares into my eyes.

Warmth eases into my hands, slowly, pushing at the fear which is making my stomach roil. His eyes are deep pools pulling me into them.

"No," I whisper. "I can't…"

"Yes, you can," he says, voice soft, barely more than a whisper.

The sound of it caresses my skin, and I shiver. He's right. I can. There's nothing here to fear. I can do this. Certainty rises, taking over my fear and pushing it out. Drawing in a deep breath, I nod.

"Right," I say. Somehow, I mean it. I can do this.

"We need to go, now," Silas says, urgently.

The ground rumbles beneath us, reminding me that we're in the middle of a trumpet sounding. Great, no time for my silly fears, we need to be under shelter. Remnants of my vision drift across my thoughts.

"Okay, let's do this," I say, gathering my nerve.

I don't know what Nathaniel did, but it helped. Efram and Rafe run over to the sorry excuse for a boat and drag it across the shore. They push it partway into the water, and I notice they watch it carefully before either of them step inside. Efram climbs in and Rafe stands to one side holding the boat.

"All aboard," Rafe says.

"Isn't that for trains?" I ask, climbing onto the boat.

My stomach clenches as it rocks back and forth under my feet. It feels weird. I can sense the water underneath me, and it doesn't feel natural. While my fears are no longer paralyzing, they are still there. Picking my way carefully, I make my way to one of the seats, sit down, and grip it with both hands.

Nathaniel and Silas climb aboard, causing the boat to rock from side to side. Instinctively, I tighten my grip, unsure what good it will do. Everyone except Rafe is on board and seated. Rafe grabs the front part of the boat and pushes us out towards the deeper water. I close my eyes, not wanting to see what happens next. There's a clattering sound, and then a splash. I open my eyes, certain that I'm about to get wet. Nathaniel, who is sitting in the middle of the boat, has an oar in each hand.

Okay, we're okay.

I look at the floor of the boat, making sure there's no

water there. It seems to be holding. Rafe leaps in, causing the boat to rock violently, and I tighten my grip, yelping.

"Sorry about that," Rafe says.

He takes a seat, and Nathaniel works the oars. The shore slides away as we move out onto the deeper water. My heart pounds, and a cold sweat trickles down my back. With each stroke, I sense the water getting deeper beneath us. It's filled with unknowns. Anything could be down there. A giant squid or some other apocalyptic horror waiting to eat us. And there's nowhere to run. We're on a boat!

No one else seems to be concerned. I wish I could emulate them. Part of me knows there's nothing here to fear, but that rational part is drowned out by the fear. Trying to take my mind off it, I look around.

It's an idyllic scene. It could be a beautiful painting for someone who had such skills. I'd buy it, if I didn't live in the Apocalypse, and if I had a home to put it in. Tall, straight pine trees ring the lake and climb the sides of the mountains.

Happy little trees, I think, laughing out loud.

Rafe glances back grinning. "A funny thought?"

"This looks like a scene that painter who used to be on TV when I was a kid would paint," I say. "You know the one, he had that really curly hair."

"Bob Ross?" Efram asks, looking around. "Yeah."

"I could see it," Rafe says.

"The happy trees guy?" Silas asks.

"Yeah, that guy," I agree. "Except... what is up with that fog?"

I point towards the shore where a thick fog is rolling towards us, fast.

"Damn," Silas mutters. "Get ready."

"Get ready for what?" I ask, but I barely get the words out before the fog envelops us.

We're floating in a sea of white.

"Row faster," Silas says, rising to his feet.

The boat rocks from side to side, and now water is splashing against it. The island has to be getting closer. Fear pounds through my veins; I'm hyperventilating. Get control, Aviella, you can't lose it like this. Obviously, we're in trouble. Stay in control.

A deafening roar sounds, so loud it hurts my ears. I can't see what's happening, but there is the sound of water bubbling. Silas utters an incantation. Sounds drift to us from all sides. It's nerve-wracking, I can't figure out which direction to look.

A tentacle erupts out of the water, swinging at us. Silas, his hands glowing with a golden light, thrusts at the incoming thing. Light bursts from his hands and explodes when it contacts it. The tentacle disintegrates.

"What is that?" I exclaim.

"They're illusions," Silas answers.

"Are you sure?" Efram asks.

"Try it," Silas answers.

Power pulses through my limbs making the hair stand on end. It's more than it ever has been before. I can feel the difference inside of me. When I take a deep breath, my lungs expand, and it feels like I'm inhaling very cold air.

More tentacles rise from the water surrounding us, waving in the air, and swinging down. Efram weaves magic and Rafe joins him. Streaks of light surge out striking tentacles, causing them to dissipate with a soft popping sound. The problem is that for every one they destroy, two more take its place.

"Row faster," Rafe says.

"I am," Nathaniel growls.

I feel helpless. Magic pulses through me, but I have no idea how to direct it in this situation. One of the tentacles slams into Silas, knocking him sideways. Rafe catches him before he goes over the side.

"I might be wrong about the illusions," Silas says, doubt in his voice.

Nathaniel is struggling to keep the oars working. Tentacles are in the way, blocking him from getting full strokes.

Aviella, a distant voice says my name. I look around but all I can see is fog and tentacles. *It's an illusion. Don't believe it!*

"Dad?" I ask.

"What's that?" Rafe asks, ducking underneath a tentacle.

I ignore him and try to focus on the soft voice that apparently only I can hear.

Disbelieve, Aviella. Disbelieve it all, Dad's voice says, sounding as if it's coming over a really bad phone connection. Tinny, distant, and almost obscured by static.

"They *are* illusions," I say out loud.

"Are you sure?" Efram asks.

"Yeah," I say.

I focus and try to see beyond the tentacles. The fog seems thinner and the more I focus, the thinner it gets. It's not real. I see that now.

Closing my eyes, I wish it all away. My magic surges and then bursts out of me in a massive pulse. When I open my eyes again, everything is normal. Rafe, Silas, and Efram look at each other before sitting down.

"Wow," Efram says, looking at me with wonder in his eyes.

"How did you know that?" Silas asks.

I bite my lip, not sure I want to say. It's probably crazy anyway. Wishful thinking or projecting my own insight onto an external source. My dad is gone. If he could reach out to me, then he should be able to find me too. Since he hasn't, I can't believe that he's talking to me.

Nathaniel looks at me over his shoulder with unreadable

eyes. I think, not for the first time, he knows something, but he's not talking about my dad. That's not frustrating, nope not at all.

Frowning I try to push my will into him, force him to say something. A tingle and then a rush passes between us. Nathaniel's eyes widen, and he jerks. He shakes his head negative before turning back around and focusing on rowing the boat.

"I'm not sure," I lie.

Now Rafe's eyes burn into me. He opens his mouth as if he's going to say something, then snaps it shut. Instead he smiles and nods.

"That's a definite increase in your power," Silas observes.

"You think?" Efram asks, sarcastically.

"I do," Silas says, ignoring or oblivious to Efram's sarcasm.

Knowing Silas, I'd go with oblivious.

The boat makes a scraping sound, and I grab my seat gasping. Looking around wildly I breathe a sigh of relief, seeing we've pulled up onto the island.

"Oh, thank God," I say.

Rafe laughs. "Told you it would be okay."

"Yeah," I say. "Excuse me for having my doubts."

Rafe leaps over the side of the boat, splashing into the water that comes up to his knees. He grabs the side and drags it further up onto the shore. The boys climb out first, and then Rafe hold his hand out for me. He helps me over the side and makes sure I'm steady on my feet.

"Well, here we are," I say.

"We need to make it up there," Silas says pointing.

A path makes its way from the beach we're standing on up through the trees towards the Bunker. It looks well-worn, as if it's been traveled a lot and probably recently. It's wide enough for us to walk three abreast if we'd like. As I follow it up towards the Bunker, I can get a better view of the structure.

It's a large, stone building, with two massive pillars set beside what looks like a steel door. Whoever built this was ready for something. The walls have black marks on them that looks like somebody tried burning it at some point. There are pock marks in the stone making me think at some point this place was sieged.

We form a loose group and walk up the path. The mood is somber, so no one is talking. My thoughts go to my dad. Is it really him? If he is talking to me, why hasn't he come and found me? I'm certain, or at least I was, that he's alive. He has to be, right? I'd feel it or something if he wasn't. I think. I hope.

I can't escape the circle of my thoughts that are consuming me. I'm barely aware of the world around me. So much as happened, so much loss, so many failures. It would be a huge win to find my dad. Just knowing he's out there safe or at least alive would take a great weight off me.

"So, do we knock?" Rafe asks.

"Seems as good as anything," Efram answers.

There are definite signs on the heavy metal door that there was some kind of a battle here. Deep gouges, burn marks, and impacts are evident. Rafe saunters forward and raises his hand to knock. Before his hand hits the door, it swings open and there's a rustling sound around us.

A man in a suit stands in the doorway with a clipboard in his hand. Flanking him on either side are heavily armed men in what looks like riot gear. Stepping out of the woods along the path are more men in similar gear, all of whom have weapons trained on us.

"Shit," I say.

CHAPTER NINETEEN

I look at Silas, mouth agape. "You said it would be safe."

"It's fine," Silas says. "Everything is as expected."

"Yes, we've been expecting you," the man with the clipboard says.

"Obviously," Rafe says, sarcastic as he looks around at the armed men. "It's also obvious that we're a very dangerous bunch."

"This is standard procedure," Clipboard Man says.

"Silas?" I ask.

"Trust me, Aviella," he says. "It will all be fine."

Efram and Nathaniel shift from foot to foot but don't say anything. I look at Rafe, and he shrugs, shaking his head negative. It's not like we have any options. Another trumpet has sounded, staying outside is beyond foolish. We need the protection of the Bunker.

"If you will all just come with me," Clipboard Man says. "I will take you to processing. We need to get you sorted."

Tingles run up and down the skin of my arms. Processing. As I've learned, that can mean so many different things depending on where you are. It doesn't sound particularly ominous said by this man, but it doesn't lessen my pullback. I don't want to be separated from the boys.

The worst part is not having a choice. We need protection in the Bunker. Frowning, I nod, and we allow ourselves to be herded through the door. Inside is a short hallway that ends in a set of steel doors.

"Is that an elevator?" I ask.

"Of course," Clipboard Man says.

He says this as if it's the most run-of-the-mill thing ever. Maybe it is, here. If there's one thing I've learned in the Apocalypse, there is no such thing as normal. The shiny steel doors slide open and we file into the box. The armed men stay behind, taking up positions to either side of the doors but even so it's crowded.

The elevator jerks into motion causing us to sway back and forth, bumping into each other in the tight quarters. I take pride in the fact that I don't yelp. At least I've got something going for me. There are no indicators to show the passing floors, so I have no idea how far down we go. At last, after what feels like a small eternity, the elevator rumbles to a stop, and the doors slide open.

Clipboard Guy walks out first and goes some distance before stopping as if he suddenly realizes we're not following. He arches an eyebrow.

"Coming?" he asks, when we don't move.

I poke my head out of the elevator and look around. It's another long hallway but this one is carpeted, with expensive-looking dark paneling on the walls. Clipboard Guy says nothing, waiting more or less patiently. There's an oppressive air to the place that I don't like. It's nothing I can put my finger on exactly, but it makes me a little uncomfortable.

"Everything will be fine," Silas says, reassuring us again. "The Dragon who runs this Bunker could not care less about you or us."

"Sounds good on paper," I mutter, stepping out. "It's not like we have a choice."

Clipboard Guy takes off again, and we follow. This hallway has heavy wooden doors, all of which are closed. There is no sound coming from behind them. There's barely the sound of us as we pass thanks to the extra-thick plush carpet. It's so thick I sink partway into it with every step. It creates a sense of luxury and excess.

The hallway turns to the left, and I see two guards waiting for us ahead. They're dressed in full riot gear like the ones above, but have their automatic weapons pointing at the floor. Clipboard Guy pulls a card out of his pocket and holds it up as he approaches. The guard on the right nods and steps to one side.

There's a keypad on the wall behind him. Clipboard Guy walks up to it, and there's the sound of buttons being pressed, although he carefully blocks our view. The two guards stare at us with cold hard eyes while he punches in the code.

"Hi," I say, smiling tentatively.

They frown deeper if that is even possible, apparently offended by my attempt to be friendly.

Jerks.

Rafe snorts and Efram steps closer, protective as ever. The door slides open with a whoosh and Clipboard Guy walks through. He doesn't wait for us or look back, so I follow, half-expecting one of these burly guards to stop me. I figure if he does, he'll be in for one hell of a surprise.

Although I brace for it nothing happens. They barely look over as we walk by. The door slides shut behind us and the air pressure changes. My ears try to pop so I yawn to ease them.

Now we're in a waiting room. The same thick carpet and dark paneling decorates the twenty-foot square room. There are chairs lining the walls on the left in the right. The wall straight ahead has wooden swinging double doors with small round windows in them.

"Central processing is through here," Clipboard Guy says. "You will need to be sorted."

"But we'll still be together, right?" I ask, looking at Silas more than Clipboard Guy.

"I cannot guarantee that," Clipboard Guy says. "Everyone is sorted by their skills and the Bunker's needs."

"No," I say, shaking my head. "We have to remain together."

"Aviella, it will all be fine. I assure you," Silas says.

Taking a deep breath, I let it out slowly. I trust him, even if I don't trust this bureaucrat. He hasn't lied to me, and I think I would know it if he did. The connection between us is very strong, and I'd be able to sense it. Besides, I don't think they're going to be doing any kind of investigation into what happened to the guy who was running Wormwood. First rule of the Bunkers is that no other Bunker matters.

I'm also certain that the Dragon who runs this Bunker couldn't care less about me. Silas has said as much, and it lines up with my impression of the Dragons when I met them.

As with most things in my life, it's not like I have a choice. I roll with the punches and do whatever it takes to survive. I know everyone around me believes I have some great destiny. I sure as hell hope they're right, otherwise what is the point of all this? I never considered myself to be special, but my life is certainly turning out to be different than I expected.

"Fine," I snap, crossing my arms over my chest and glaring. "Let's get this over with."

Clipboard Guy smiles and nods. "Follow me, please."

The worst thing you can do to somebody who is trying to give you a death stare is act like nothing's happening. I decide I like this guy even less than I did.

As a group we walk through the wooden double doors that swing silently open on well-oiled hinges.

Emerging on the other side is like stepping into a massive factory.

The carpet is gone as we step out onto a concrete floor. Bright yellow stripes demarcate walking paths stretching off as far as I can see. There are white offices lining the walkway on the left and right, each one a small, stand-alone building with a single door and a window that has soft light streaming out.

Guards are on duty every few hundred feet, all in full riot gear with weapons resting casually in front of them. In front of each office there is a bench with several people sitting there. They look like survivors. Dirty, torn clothes. Faraway looks on their faces. The guards watch them carefully.

The bench to my left has a family sitting on it, a mom and dad with a little girl who looks like she might be five or six years old. She's playing with a rag doll that is missing an eye. The parents have a shell-shocked look, but the girl seems happy enough. How happy can you be in the Apocalypse?

"You are to be given priority treatment," Clipboard Guy says.

"Priority?" I ask, looking at the family to my left.

"Yes, of course," he says, his eyes on Silas.

"What about them?" I ask. "How long have they been waiting?"

"I don't see where that is any of your concern," Clipboard Guy says.

"Aviella," Silas says, stepping into my view.

"No," I say. "Why should we be given priority over them? They have a child. They need shelter."

Silas stares into my eyes without saying a word. His mouth opens, and I expect him to argue, but he snaps it shut. He turns back to the Clipboard Guy and whispers something that I can't make out. Clipboard Guy shakes his head negative, points at his board, but Silas continues talking. In a moment Clipboard Guy shoulders slump, and I see him visibly give in.

"Of course," Clipboard Guy says. "I will see to it immediately."

He walks into the nearest office, closing the door behind him and leaving the five of us standing in a loose circle. A thrill of victory buoys my spirits. If I've learned anything it's to take whatever minor victories you can when they come along. In my life they've been rare enough to be treasured.

"We shouldn't rock the boat anymore," Silas says. "It wasn't easy getting us placement here."

"Okay," I say, feeling magnanimous after my victory.

"We ran to get away from the Dragons," Nathaniel says. "Now we are under one of their thumbs."

"I understand," Silas says, in his trademark answering without answering way.

Clipboard Guy reappears and the family waiting on the bench brighten when he stops in front of them. They file into the office, and I want to do a victory dance. He then walks over to us.

"Follow me please," he says, without further ado.

Having claimed my small victory, I follow without further argument.

"You will be processed in here," Clipboard Guy says, pointing to one of the offices.

I look at each of my men, swallowing hard. Fear grips my guts. I should be honest with myself about how much I want them. I don't just want them, I need them. They're integral to me, a part of me.

Steeling my nerves, I turn and walk into the office.

CHAPTER TWENTY

*T*he intake process seems to go relatively fast, for a Bunker. I'm sort of used to these. I've been given all the proper paperwork and told to wait outside the office. Apparently a staffer will be here to show me around soon.

I look around outside hoping to see at least one of the guys, but none of them are out yet. It's only a few minutes later when Silas walks out of one of the offices. A young person is with him who is all but tripping over himself in his efforts to be overly deferential.

"I am so sorry," the young man says, pushing his hair back out of his face. He has one of those haircuts where it is cut short on the sides and long on the top, but it keeps falling into his eyes. "Somehow it was missed you had arrived."

"It's fine," Silas says dismissively as he looks around. His eyes land on me and he smiles.

What is up with this? I wonder.

"No, sir, it's not. I assure you there will be an investigation into how this happened, and it will not happen again."

"Thank you," Silas says.

"If you want to follow me now," the young man says.

Silas is barely paying attention to him. He's staring at me like he's undressing me with his eyes. My cheeks warm under his gaze and warmth spreads through my belly. His sharp eyes, strong jaw, and lithe physique intrigue me. Despite the distance between us, I feel his energy reach out to me. A shudder runs down my spine. My imagination runs wild, and I feel his lips exploring my skin. My cheeks flush hotter. Could I be any more inappropriate?

Silas smiles, a knowing smile. He turns away and the moment is broken. The staffer leads him around the corner and I lose sight of them. As I watch him disappear, I'm certain I'll be seeing him before long. The only question then is, can I keep restraining myself around him?

I don't see any sign of the other guys. They must still be in processing, which is ridiculous if Silas and I are both out. The guards don't appear to be watching me with any particular interest, so I'm left on my own, waiting. Surely, they won't leave me hanging for long, will they?

"Excuse me?"

I jump at the sudden voice, whirling around to face a young girl. She's dressed in a gray uniform, like the staffer I saw with Silas, and a smile. She's young and bright-eyed, with the sides of her head shaved and the top part long, hanging down almost to her eyes, similar to the other one I saw. It must be the style here in Bunker 3.

"Yeah," I say, waiting for my heart to come down out of my throat.

"Would you follow me please?"

"Uh, okay," I say, looking at the offices up and down the row. "Are my friends coming?"

She looks at the clipboard in her hand before answering.

"I'm sure they'll be along soon," she smiles.

"That's not an answer," I say.

"I'm sorry, I don't have any information on them right

now," she says, smiling bigger. "But sometimes we're a bit slow taking people in. You know how it can be. We don't want just anyone coming in here."

"Why not?" I ask, feeling obstinate but also genuinely curious. Her eyes widen in surprise.

"Well, because we're unique," she says.

"In what way? It's a Bunker, like any other," I say.

"Oh no," she says, shaking her head, face alight with pride. "We're not like any other Bunker. We have one of the only unpolluted sources of water left. We're unique and very important to the future survival of our race."

"I see," I say, shaking my head. "So, you hoard water and what, exploit it in trade with other Bunkers?"

"We do not exploit," she says, pursing her lips. "Fair trade is very important."

"Of course, it is," I agree, sighing heavily because I know fair doesn't mean what I think it does.

Her jaw tightens as she purses her lips and her brow furrows. Tapping the clipboard against her leg she stares at me, and I see she's debating her response.

"It is," she says, indignant. "We're not like the other Bunkers. Something we take great pride in."

"I see that," I say, failing to keep the sarcasm out of my voice.

Her cheeks flush red and her mouth opens, then snaps shut. She shakes her head before turning and walking.

"Follow me please," she says.

I didn't mean to offend her, but obviously I have. Now I feel bad about it. Rushing to catch up to her, I try to think of an appropriate way to say I'm sorry. She doesn't look over, arms swinging in time with the rhythm of her legs as she rushes down hallways. It's all I can do to keep up with her.

"I'm sorry," I say, opting for the easiest. "I wasn't trying to offend you."

She slows her pace, but doesn't stop. I wait for any other sign of her forgiveness and at last she sighs and glances over.

"It's fine," she says. "I thought you would be different."

She thought I would be different? What does she know about me? Why would I be any different than anyone else?

Fear makes a cold knot in my belly. Being known isn't a good thing, ever.

"What do you mean?" I ask, doing my damnedest to make it seem casual.

"Well, you're special, of course," she says. "Why else would Lord Tynan take an interest in you?"

"Oh, he's taken an interest in me?" I ask, feigning more surprise than I feel.

That's good, go casual me. It's the best way to hide the cold chills running down my limbs.

"Sure," she says, curiosity in her voice.

We're walking through a crowded marketplace. There are a lot of people around. Everyone is well-dressed, well fed, and obviously well-to-do. It's not like the Bunker I grew up in. This is a high-end area, and I wonder if all of the Bunker is like this. If so, then it's definitely different.

The hairs on the back of my neck are standing on end, and although I can't point to anyone directly it feels like all their eyes are on me. Out of the corner of my eye people shoot dirty looks in my direction. I don't know what's up with that. I haven't been here long enough to cause a problem. I can't imagine that my reputation has proceeded me this far.

"I didn't realize he knew I existed," I lie. "Why would he possibly have an interest in me?"

I feign confusion, considering it's probably the best avenue for me at this point. I don't want to give away too much. She gives me a sideways glance as if trying to decide whether I'm lying or stupid. Stupid is better for me, so I smile broadly doing my best to appear idiotic.

"I'm sure you'll find out soon," she says, which is almost as good of a non-answer as Silas would give.

She leads us further and further into the Bunker. The walls here are not bare stone or concrete like every other Bunker I've been in, they're covered with dark wood panels. The halls are all carpeted with thick plush. The entire effect is quite nice and luxurious.

The crowds aren't as thick as they were but there are still people moving up and down hallways and they're still giving me dirty looks. Well, I guess I didn't come here to make friends.

Turning into yet another hallway, we're halfway down it when I notice runes carved into the walls. Stopping I walk over and trace the outlines with my fingers. Some of these I recognize from my vision, the ones we still can't translate.

"What are these?" I ask.

"I don't know," she answers. "They've always been here."

"Someone must know," I say, insisting.

"Lord Tynan might," she says.

Great, the one person here I don't want to see is the one with the answers. As it turns out I may not have much choice but to interact with the Dragon, again. Well, I don't know why I'm surprised, this is the way my life goes.

We carry on our way, all the while getting the dirty looks, but I don't care. Let them look. They have no idea of what I've seen or what I've had to do. They're worried about their small, petty lives, when the fate of the world literally hangs in the balance.

She stops at a door and pulls out a key. It isn't a key card like most places would have but an actual, physical key. That's different, and something I haven't seen in a long time. She puts it in the door, and it clicks loudly then the door swings open silently. She walks in and I follow, my mouth agape at what I see.

The room is dominated by a large fourposter bed replete with a canopy. A velvet red comforter covers it and pillows are piled all around. There's a dresser made of real wood, stained a gorgeous cherry color. It has a massive mirror with brass accents around it. On the other side of the room there's an armoire, also real wood and stained the same. Tucked in the corner is a makeup station. The floor is covered with thick, plush carpet.

"Your private bath is through that door," she says pointing.

I have to consciously think to snap my jaw shut. I've never seen anything like this. The level of luxury is unheard of. I'm not sure that the richest people in Bunker E247 had rooms like this. The idea of a private bathroom excites me so much that I run over to the door and throw it open. Turning slowly back to face her I shake my head.

"Does everyone here live like this?" I ask.

"Not all," she says, her voice dismissive but something passes behind her eyes.

"Then why am I being treated special?" I ask, suspicion rising to the fore.

"Because he ordered it so," she says. Cold spreads throughout my body. "There are clothes for you in the armoire. He is expecting you for dinner tonight."

"You're kidding me," I say stomach knotting.

She stares at me as if I've gone insane. It makes for very long, awkward moment. Admittedly, I'm used to feeling awkward, but the disbelief in her stare makes me uncomfortable.

"Okay, fine," I say, at last to break the silence between us. "I'll get ready now."

"Good," she says, giving no sign that she intends to leave.

"Can I have some privacy?" I ask, wondering if I'm a guest or a prisoner.

Dammit Silas, you said this would be okay.

"Oh," she says, seemingly in surprise. "Of course. How long do you need?"

I glance over my shoulder at that luxurious bathroom which has a tub big enough for at least six to sit comfortably. I'm betting it also has water jets, and doesn't that sound nice?

"A couple of hours?" I ask, a sly grin on my face.

"Not a problem," she says, walking towards the door. "I'll come back for you."

"Thank you," I say.

As soon as the door shuts behind her, I strip and head for the bathroom. First rule of the Apocalypse, take advantage of every good thing that comes along. They are rare and precious, and the memory of them will help you get through the bad times.

CHAPTER TWENTY-ONE

The dress I'm wearing is uncomfortable as hell, even though it fits perfectly. I try not to think about that too much, because how did they know my exact size? Whatever, I'm not going to worry about it.

The dress itches and is pinching me around my waist. It keeps wanting to ride up. It's obviously designed for a formal evening out. It's a strapless number that reveals more of my chest than I'm comfortable with. As I look myself over in the mirror. I turn from one side to the other trying to get a full view, and despite my overall discomfort, I like the way I look. It makes me feel sexy.

As soon as I open my door, the staffer is waiting. Her eyes widen, and she smiles broadly, nodding appreciatively.

"He's going to like that," she says.

I'm not sure how I feel about that. Butterflies dance in my stomach. I'm not sure I want him to like anything about me. He's a Dragon, one of the Horsemen, not the kind of being I want to attract attention from. At the same time, having met him, part of me does. A deep, dirty part that I don't want to admit to, but it is there.

Conflicted, I follow her as she leads the way through the halls. It doesn't take me long to figure out we're going up. The further we go, the more often I see guards on duty until at last we come to a large hallway with two guards posted at its entrance. They don't pay any attention to us as we walk by, not even so much as a nod.

At the end of the hallway, there are two glass French doors that look out onto a beautiful scene. I see the mountain range through floor-to-ceiling windows beyond a perfectly arranged garden filled to the brim with flowers and greenery. She opens the door to let me through. The scent of life is overwhelming as I step through. It's not unpleasant, actually it's incredibly nice, as if the very smells have been picked to make sure they complement each other.

We're in a sunroom. Perfectly clear glass ceiling and walls protect us from the elements. We walk along a path lined with tables displaying the various plants and flowers. When we turn another corner, I pause. The view takes my breath away.

It looks out over a section of the lake. Everything is perfect. Looking at this, you would never know that the Apocalypse had happened.

"You like the view?" Tynan says, walking over.

Tearing my eyes away and looking at him, my heart leaps into my throat and my stomach sinks to the floor. He oozes sex, it drips off him. He walks with a swagger that announces his confidence and certainty. He dominates the space and everyone in it. I lose myself in his easy smile, his sparkling eyes, and his stunning physique.

A fire rages in my core as my lady bits inflame with unsuppressed desire. My mouth is dry, too dry to swallow, I can't form words. I have to respond, say something, anything.

"Huh-uh-I-uhba-yeah," I stutter, my cheeks flushing red-hot with embarrassment.

Tynan laughs and even that, though it's at my own expense, is over-the-top sexy. I want to throw myself at him. I want him to take me and use me. Right here, right now.

Get a grip, Aviella, I yell at myself.

He steps to one side and makes a motion with his arm, drawing my eyes away from him, for which I'm thankful. A small table with a white cloth on it sits by one of the glass walls. We walk side by side over to it and he holds out my chair for me, pushing it in like a perfect gentleman. The table takes full advantage of the beautiful view, but now all of my attention is on him.

He sits across from me and the servant comes up holding a pad in his hand. Tynan stares at me with an easy, sexy smile.

"Your orders?" the servant asks, looking at me.

"The lady will have the salmon," Tynan says before I can speak. "Start her off with the house salad, pair it with an appropriate wine. We'll decide on dessert later."

His eyes tell me everything I need to know. He's playing with me. This is a game to him. In any other situation I'd be offended, and I'd let it be well-known, but in this case, I decide to play along. I nod to the servant, granting my agreement.

"Thank you," I say to Tynan.

He smiles and shrugs as if it's nothing.

"I'm so glad you made your way here. I had half a mind to go out looking for you," he says.

I smile uncertainly. I can see the complement, but I'm not happy being the center of his attention. I don't know what to make of it. I've grown comfortable and accustomed to Rafe and the guys. When I'm with them it feels like we've known each other much longer than we have. Dragons are another matter.

I can't forget they are the ones who run the Bunker societies. The politics, the infighting, the struggling to survive all stems from them. How trustworthy can they be if they run places like this?

"You are tempting me to read your thoughts. I hope you'll offer them instead," he says.

Shit, I think. Dragons *can* read minds. As many times as I've wondered about Rafe I don't think he can. The one sitting across from me, this Dragon, absolutely can.

"It's been a long trip —," I say.

"Say no more," Tynan smiles. "I won't keep you up past your bedtime... tonight."

There's no mistaking the way he tacked on the word tonight. Worst part of that is I can't deny how good an offer like that from Tynan would be. I'm not sure I could say no, or that I'd want to. There's been so much sexual tension between the guys and me, and now to add in the Dragon?

It's starting to feel like I'm nothing more than a raw, sexual hive of nerves. A girls gotta get some relief at some point.

Mentally I exert control of myself and try to tuck away any hint of my desires. I don't know how well it works, because I see he feels my interest. The way he looks at me, I feel vulnerable and want to run back to my room and hide.

"Thank you," I say, deciding to respond to the words he said, and ignore the implications. "I am quite tired."

"You're probably wondering about your friends. I'm sure they'll be around soon. They have access to the lower lounges."

The lower lounges, got it, I think. Something must show on my face, or else he is reading my thoughts.

"Only the very special ones frequent the higher halls, dear. Tradition dies hard, even in Bunker society."

"Tradition flows from —" I start to snap, but I'm interrupted by the dreaded sound of hooves.

It's the horsemen of the Army that was released with the last trumpet. I feel them stampeding across the earth, leaving destruction in their path. Cold fear races down my spine and the hair on the back of my neck stands on end. I look around trying to spot the source.

"It's they who should fear us," Tynan says, smiling and certain. "When I hunt with my brothers, I serve up trumpet–fare for our most special affairs."

I control my facial reactions, remembering Silas social lessons he put me through.

He's completely serious. Of course he is... he's a Dragon.

CHAPTER TWENTY-TWO

EFRAM

"This isn't what we agreed to," I say.

"No, not exactly," Rafe says. "But it doesn't change the situation. We have to do what's best for Aviella."

"We could start with knowing exactly where she is, right now," I say, frustration mounting.

"We should go out exploring," Nathaniel says. "Get the lay of the land."

"Silas said she would be taken to the upper levels," Rafe adds. "Nothing is different than what we expected."

Closing my eyes, I take a deep breath and count to ten. I have a wild urge to punch the demon in the face. It's not his fault I'm frustrated. I want to find Aviella. I need to see her, to know for sure she's okay.

"Fine," I say, getting control myself at last. "I'm going out to explore. Maybe I can drum up some work."

"That's a good idea," Nathaniel says, nodding his head.

The angel isn't any better than the demon. It pisses me off that they both seem calm. I know I can trust Silas, but it doesn't make it any easier to be separated from her. Another trumpet has sounded, and I should be at her side.

Rather than argue further, I walk out of the small, shared bunk we've been assigned. We're in the lower levels, as they call them here. Everyone is dressed in drab gray coveralls and rushes from one place to another. I fall in with a group heading towards something. They barely give me a side glance.

"What's the rush?" I ask.

"We have to hurry up and prepare," one of them says, glancing over.

"Prepare for what?" I ask.

The leader of the group looks over his shoulder, frowning deeply. "Are you kidding?"

"No?" I give him my best smile.

"The contest is only two days away," he snaps. "Who do you think does all the set-up work? Who do you think makes sure it goes off without a hitch? It doesn't take care of itself."

"I see," I say, nodding. "Well I'm sure your hard work is appreciated."

"The only thing our hard work matters for is, it gives us an opportunity to compete," another one of the group answers. "I'm going to be selected this time. I'm sure of it."

"Selected for what?" I ask, a cold ball of ice forming in my stomach.

"To be one of the Darlings, of course," the same one answers me. "You aren't from around here, are you?"

"Why are you following us?" the leader asks, glaring. "Don't you have anything better to do?"

"I'll be going on my way now," I say, dropping away from the group and letting them run on.

Interesting. I can infer from what I gathered there that they have some kind of regular contest giving the lower-Bunkers an opportunity to move up into the higher-Bunkers. I pass the rest of the day listening and asking questions. It's not the worst system that I've seen. As with most of the

Bunkers, the society here is cutthroat. By their very nature, it's hard to have them be any other way.

There's a limited number of resources to be shared among all inhabitants. The laws of supply and demand cause some to rise to the top while others suffer. That's the nature of man. As an educated guess, the contest for the Darlings is as much about dangling hope in front of the worker class than an actual advancement. I'd be curious to find out what happens to those who "win." There's part of me that doesn't want to know.

I've spent enough time on this and decide to head back and see what Rafe and Nathaniel have found out.

CHAPTER TWENTY-THREE

a s I walk away from the dinner with Tynan my skin is on fire. The pulsing need and burning desires cloud my thoughts. One way or another, I've got to get some relief soon. It's a terrible situation to be in. So many handsome men, all interested, all wanting me, but not a damn one of them will act. Sooner or later, this house of cards has to come tumbling down. It's only a matter of who's going to make the first move.

I'm just not sure how long I can wait. A girl's got needs.

My thoughts are consumed by the dinner. Tynan is arrogant yet sexy, confident—and yet behind that I felt a vulnerability. That vulnerability drew me in like a moth to a flame. I want to unwrap his hard exterior and find that soft center.

I'm more than willing to admit I also want to unwrap the package of his body. I have no doubts of its perfection.

No, Aviella, get a grip. I need to push past this. What can I do?

"I'd like to see my friends now," I say to the staffer leading me through the hallways.

"I don't think they've come out of processing yet," she says, clearly dodging the request.

"Why is it taking so long?" I ask.

She stops, turning towards me with a now-familiar fixed smile.

"The upper levels are not for everyone. I'm afraid they are not welcome here, and at this point in time it would be very bad for you to go to them. So, they are not currently available," she says, keeping that fixed smile, but behind her eyes there's something much more dangerous.

I debate her words. I want to smash her face in and make her take me to them. Lucky for her, I'm trying to be more mature and in better control, like Silas taught me. Silas, that's an idea.

"Then take me to Silas," I say.

I see the debate raging in her eyes as she tries to find some reason to not take me to him too. I have to wonder, are these Tynan's orders? Is he trying to keep me separated from my friends? If he is, why?

"Of course," she acquiesces.

I follow her, doing my best to remember the various turns we take as I try to learn the layout of this new Bunker. We go down one level by stairs before we get to his place. She motions to a door without saying a word.

"I'll find my own way home," I say, smiling.

"Of course," she says, nodding at last. I'm not leaving her a lot of room. If she was to argue further, it would become more than obvious I'm not a guest. If nothing else, I know Tynan doesn't want me to think that, no matter what the case may be.

I watch her leave before I raise a hand to knock on the door.

CHAPTER TWENTY-FOUR

SILAS

"*A*viella," I say, in surprise.

Her energy hits me like a crashing wave. Instantly I'm swept up in its embrace, surrounded as it drags me under. Involuntarily, I step back. The power of her emotions and the fire in her eyes takes me by surprise. She's wearing a beautiful evening gown that accents her perfect curves and reveals more of her chest than I've seen. I can't keep my eyes off that bare skin.

"Silas," she says, a tentative smile on her face.

My eyes are drawn to her full lips, and lust rages to life, filling me. Her sweet lips, burnings eyes, luscious body —all call to me. The urge to claim her consumes me, burning at my self-control.

"Come in," I say, stepping to one side and motioning.

It's hard to form words. My thoughts are a wild storm of emotions and desire. My own magical energy entwines with hers, twisting and turning together in the same way my body wants to meld with hers. My control is slipping, something that hasn't happened in ages. Physically, blood rushes to the one part of me that I don't want to be getting any extra right now. It adds to the distraction.

She walks past, hips swaying as she moves. Is that an extra bit of swing? The flow of her steps, the way her ass moves up and down, the curve of her side… STOP!

Control. I am in control.

I tear my eyes away. Walking past her, pointedly not looking, I go over to the small bar that came with my room. Pulling out two glasses is routine, normal, and it focuses my attention.

"Would you like some water?" I ask, holding up the crystal decanter so that it catches the light, causing a prism spray.

Looking at the rainbow effect is sufficiently distracting to keep my attention. It helps.

"Please," she says, her voice low and husky.

I pour water for both of us. It's pure, fresh water that hasn't been filtered and re-filtered, unlike any of the other Bunkers. Bunker 3 has the only pure source left on the planet. It's untainted by radiation or other side-effects of the Apocalypse.

As I do, she makes herself at home, sitting down on the overstuffed couch and pulling her legs up under her. Avoiding direct eye-contact, I hand her the glass then take a seat across from her. Desire pulses off her in pounding waves. It's like a driving bass line at an overly loud concert. Assaulting my defenses instead of my eardrums, but the analogy is a good one.

"Is everything okay?" I ask.

"Yes," she says, swirling the tumbler of water. "No, maybe."

She shakes her head, not meeting my eyes.

"What's happened?" I ask, leaning forward, drawn in by her.

"I had dinner with Tynan," she says, not looking up.

That explains a lot. The Dragons have this effect on women. It's part of their nature, a supernatural effect. A stabbing pain drives into my heart, and I barely suppress a grimace.

"How did that go?" I ask, carefully schooling my face and voice.

I have to know—but I don't want to. I want her, for myself, not to share with a being like one of the Dragons. If he claimed her... I'll what? Tynan is a Horsemen, a Dragon like all of them, but more than that. What right do I have to her? She gives me what she decides; I am not in control of her.

"Interesting," she says. "He's different..."

"Different?" I ask, encouraging her to keep talking.

"Yes, powerful, of course," she says, musing. Suddenly her eyes lock on mine, and my heart soars as my breath catches in my chest. "There's more to him than meets the eye. Something deeper, a part he doesn't show the world."

"I see," I say, breathless, consumed by her lips and my desire to taste them.

"Or maybe he's playing me," she says, looking away and breaking the moment. "I don't know."

"I'm working on him," I say. "He has texts even more ancient than any I or the mages do, I'm trying to gain access. I hope to find more information on the symbols you've seen."

She nods, distracted and obviously not wanting to change the subject. When she looks at me again, desire burns hot in her eyes. Slowly, sensually, she rises from the couch. Setting the tumbler down on the coffee table, she lingers in that bent-over position. Her breasts sway under the thin cloth. My mouth waters and my cock stiffens, harder than steel.

She moves around the table, desire given form. Pausing in

front of me she places a leg on each side of mine than slowly leans in towards me. I should stop this. I should... but I can't.

Her lips close with mine. I struggle for control but the scent of her is intoxicating, heady, like the best of drinks. Rarified air that has to be breathed to appreciate.

Her eyes burn with desire, consuming me with her fire, as her lips and body move closer. Her breasts touch my chest, my cock pulses in time with my pounding heart.

"Thank you," she exhales, her sweet breath warming my skin.

She's been through so much, and she has needs. We all do. It will be okay if I give in. Our lips touch. Hers are soft, full, and lush with a hint of raspberry. She moans softly when I return her kiss. My hands move to her sides, fingers tingling with delight as I touch her curves, sliding them down towards her perfect ass.

Her tongue darts out, seeking mine, and I welcome it.

Lust. Pure. Unadulterated.

No. I can't, I won't. Not like this.

She's too special. This is not the way I will have her.

I pull back.

She pushes forward, trying to claim her desire, but I sink further into the overstuffed chair keeping the small distance between us. Disappointment flares in her eyes as her face falls, her lips forming a frown. The look on her face is a more direct assault on my control than anything that has happened so far. It takes all my will to hold onto it.

"It's late, lovely girl," I say. "I'll escort you to your quarters."

She rises, straightening her dress.

"Of course," she says, her cheeks flushing a delicate pink.

Standing, I take her hand, silently, pushing away my own regrets as I struggle internally to keep control and do what I know is right. We walk out in tense silence but by the time we reach her hallway the tension is gone between us. She unlocks her door, and I wait until she steps inside. She turns, leaning against the door, meeting my eyes at last.

"Thank you," she says, her voice soft, eyes demure.

The overwhelming nature of my feelings for her rages, swelling to fill me and pouring out. I will do anything for her. I am hers, truly and fully. Including this: I will give her away if that is what she wants. The bond between us is that strong.

I smile to cover the emotional storm raging inside and nod, unable to form words.

She closes the door. I wait until I hear the turning of the locks before walking away.

CHAPTER TWENTY-FIVE

*G*od, I've made a fool of myself! What was I thinking!

Storming around my room, I tear off the dress, almost ripping the delicate fabric as I struggle to get out. The zipper catches and won't budge no matter how I tug.

"Damn it!"

Breathe, calm down

Shaking my head, I close my eyes and inhale deeply, holding it. Letting the breath out slowly I open my eyes then reach behind myself and methodically work the zipper. It releases at last, and I slide out of the dress.

Walking into the full bath I turn on the shower. In moments steam is billowing and the mirror is fogging over. I step under the hot water. It beats down on my back, and the tension starts to ease.

It's not that bad. Right? He returned the kiss, and there isn't any doubt whatsoever he wanted me. There was no mistaking the bulge in his pants...

Nope, I'm a fool.

Throwing myself at Silas like some kind of hussy. What

the hell was I thinking? Idiot. What would Efram, Rafe, and Nathaniel think? What would Tynan think?

Why do I care?

Who am I to have problems like this?

Ugh, stop!

Circling my thoughts like this will get me nowhere. I know this too well from my time in the orphanage. I was an outcast then with no friends. Damn, I miss Rowan.

How long has it been since she left?

I've barely had time to think about her, but it's times like this that her infectious smile and mime antics would lift my spirits. Make me feel less like a fool. I need that.

She's with the mages, safe. I hope anyway. In theory, she's safe. Safer than she would be with me, obviously. I attract attention, too much of it. Dragons taking an interest in me? What next?

I let the water run over my face, and the tension finally drops away. My thoughts quit circling. Thank you, Rowan. Even when you're not here, you're my best friend.

I want to see the boys. Rafe is almost as good as Rowan at lifting my spirits. Almost, but not quite. He would be every bit as good, I'm sure, if it wasn't for the attraction between the two of us. Running my fingers through my hair, rinsing out the soap, that thought blossoms bright.

How, in the name of all that's holy, am I supposed to balance this? There's no denying the attraction between me and each of the guys. It's visceral, real, magnetic, and a dozen other adjectives I can't think of. Each one of them has a hold on me but each in their own, unique way that is distinctly them.

If I was to do something with one of them, what would that do to the others? I don't want to hurt any of them. I want all of them. Damn, I'm greedy I guess, but how would that ever work?

I don't know.

I do know it feels right. There's something about it that makes the universe click into place, as if this is the way it's supposed to be.

I turn off the water, step out, and dry off. I wipe the steam off the mirror so I can stare at myself, dripping wet, hair plastered to my head.

"What are you thinking?" I ask myself.

Unfortunately, I don't answer myself.

CHAPTER TWENTY-SIX

NATHANIEL

Following a feeling, I walk the halls of the lower levels of Bunker 3. Something pulls me along. It's instinctual, but that's often how my abilities work. A feeling, an idea, never a clear-cut "Do this." God doesn't work that way. Even Angels have a semblance of free will.

There are specials here, somewhere. I'm not sure if I'm supposed to find them, but if I am meant to, I will. Of that I'm certain.

It gives me something to focus on besides her. Anything is a welcome distraction from the all-consuming nature of my attraction to her. I need this, welcome it. It keeps me from storming the upper levels to find her. Which would be a bad, no, a stupid-bad idea.

Irritating the Dragon isn't a good idea. He's a Horseman, after all. His powers aren't something I want to go toe-to-toe against.

Passing by a vent, I catch a hint of magic. Closing my eyes and expanding my senses, I scan for it. It's gray magic, coming from...

Somewhere.

Images flash as I follow the hints of it. There.

Path firmly set in my thoughts, I follow it. As I get closer I hear voices.

"It's high time we act," a male voice says. "We've got enough power."

"You think so? You really want to wake the Dragon?" another man asks.

"No," a female says. "Don't be stupid. Keep a low profile, keep working, wait for our time."

"I'm tired of waiting," the first voice says.

They stop talking when I turn the corner. It's a small Coven, six of them. I'm not sure what discipline they ascribe to, but I can sense the neutral nature of their magic, meaning they could go to either side. Unusual to find since the Apocalypse. Almost all the witches have been enticed to one side or the other.

"Can we help you?" the second male voice asks.

He's in his twenties, but his face has several scars marring it, and his eyes are hard, making it clear he's seen a lot. I'd guess he survived outside for some time before arriving here.

"No," I say. "Passing through, sorry to interrupt."

They stare at me, suspicious, and rightly so. Talk like this wouldn't be well-received by anyone on the upper levels. I'm not sure why I don't make myself known, but it doesn't feel right. It's not time.

"Then move along," the female says.

She's older, in her fifties with gray at her temples and heavy crow's-feet around her eyes. The sadness weighs her down and calls to me. I want to lift that weight for her, but I don't. Something stops me.

"Right," I say. "Sorry to interrupt."

Their glares burn into my back as I walk away. I need to get back to the others and talk to them about these witches. They might be helpful. I have to make sure everything is in place before I take off. Protecting Aviella is primary in my thoughts, above my duty to the higher calling I serve.

Once I'm out in the world, I can find the lay of the land and hopefully recruit some fresh allies. A dull ache forms in my chest, and it's hard to get a deep breath as I think about it. Leaving her behind is the last thing I want, but it's what I must do. I can't protect her without knowing what's happening out there.

Her face drifts through my thoughts. Those full, lush, raspberry lips. I desperately want to kiss them. I've never experienced anything like what she makes me feel. My desire for her is overwhelming, more so at some times than others. I want to kiss her, but I won't. When I do, it has to be right. Kissing her before leaving when there's a solid chance I won't make it back is cruel. Something I could never do to her.

A day passes by uneventfully. I venture out from my assigned room and explore, getting a feel for the Bunker. It's not fun at all. The dirty looks I get are constant. I'm not sure what I did to piss everyone off, but they're all angry at me.

I continue exploring out of obstinateness, if nothing else. The only people that I don't get dirty looks from are those in the drab gray uniforms, the 'worker' class as they're known. The 'upper' class are very busy doing nothing productive. That alone would drive me nuts, but they take it to extremes that rubs me wrong.

Parties seem to be their main business. Well that and critiquing each other and the parties someone else has thrown and everything that was wrong with it. What a waste of life. The world is a mess, they have power and resources that they could be using to help others, but instead they're wasting their time and lives on this.

Sitting by myself in a corner of the dining hall, I listen to the conversations going on. I'm ignored for the most part, though I can't help but notice the occasional stink eye thrown my way. No one wants to talk to me, which is fine. I don't have anything nice to say if they did. First time I came here for dinner, I tried being friendly, reaching out to others. I was rebuffed harder than I've ever been before, which is saying something. Since then I've kept to myself.

I've got plenty to think about. Silas, for one. Efram, Rafe, and Nathaniel for seconds. Let's not even start in with Tynan. I haven't seen Silas since I made a fool of myself in his room. I'm not sure I can face him yet.

I want to see the rest of the boys. I miss them. Efram would have some wise words for me, Rafe would make me laugh, and Nathaniel would drop some tidbit of wisdom out of nowhere. I know they're okay, but that doesn't make me feel any better. I don't want them to just be okay, I want them with me. Here, now.

Lost in my thoughts, I almost miss the change in the room. The quiet conversations shift, and the feeling in the air is different, pulling me out of my thoughts. When I look up from my food, I spot the problem. Silas is walking towards me, a smile on his face.

They're all looking from him to me, then back to him again. Whispers fly between them, and I know they're gossiping about the two of us. My cheeks warm. I don't like being the center of attention like this. It brings back too many childhood memories.

"I've been given permission to escort you to the lower level," he says, by way of greeting.

"Escort?" I ask, arching an eyebrow. I've been asking to see the boys constantly.

"Yes, an escort is customary for preferred guests," he says, shrugging as if to say it's not his rules.

The whispering becomes a storm. Great, Silas, way to fuel the rumor-mongering. I'm sure that will make my life easier. Ugh.

"Fine," I say, glad to have an excuse, any excuse, to get the hell out of here.

I grab my tray and take it up to the window to turn it in. As I walk through the tables of the well-to-do, their eyes watching me surreptitiously, I can't resist. Swinging my hips more than I normally would, I link arms with Silas, leaning against him as we walk. When we reach the doorway I stop, turn to him, and press my lips to his.

It's not passionate, unlike last time, strictly for show, but he plays into it, picking up on my cue. His hands roam down to my ass, cupping it softly, and in that instant the kiss becomes real. Full of pent-up desire and the need that we're both feeling. His body responds, digging into my stomach. Breaking the kiss, I hold eye contact with him for a moment before taking his hand and walking away.

The room is dead silent. Perfect. That will give them something to talk about.

Silas walks with me in silence, and only after we've gone quite a distance does the embarrassment hit me. What did I do?

"Uh, sorry," I mutter.

"For?" he asks.

"That… display. They're pissing me off."

"Well, if that's how you deal with being pissed off, then I'd like to see you angry more often."

I glance over, trying to get a handle on his mood, but his face is dead serious. He holds that face for a long moment, almost long enough for me to buy it, before a shit-eating grin breaks out.

"You did give them something. I'm sure that will be the topic of discussion for at least a month," he laughs.

I match his grin, nodding.

"Screw them," I say. "I hate this class-ism crap. We're all people, we should be helping each other."

"I agree, in principle. They're clinging to anything, trying to keep themselves sane. While it doesn't make it right, and I don't agree with it, I do understand it," he says, turning it into a teaching moment.

Of course he would do that. He's Silas. It's a big part of what I love about him.

We talk this over as we make our way to the lower levels. We're so deep in the discussion I almost don't notice Efram walking out of a room. Almost but not quite.

"Efram!" I exclaim.

He wheels around, eyes widening, mouth dropping open. He's dripping with sweat and his hair is plastered to his head, but I don't care. I run for him and leap when I'm still ten feet away. He catches me in his arms easily, pulling me into a tight embrace against him. Damn he smells good, even if he's all sweaty. It's musky and manly. His muscles bulge as he squeezes me. He sets me on my feet and we part, slowly separating, when suddenly I'm swept off my feet and spinning.

"AVIELLA!" Rafe exclaims, holding me in the air and twirling me.

"Rafe!" I laugh, getting dizzy.

We're attracting attention, a lot of it. Dozens of people in worker-drab gray are staring, mouths agape, at our public display of affection.

"We should take this inside," Efram says, tapping Rafe on the shoulder.

"You're a party pooper," Rafe grouses. "Let them look, I'll give them a show they won't forget."

He pulls me close, and then his lips are on mine. His tongue invades my mouth aggressively as both his hands find my ass. I give myself over to the kiss, wrapping my arms around his neck and pulling him as tight to me as I am to him.

When we part at last due to the demands of air, he laughs, long and loud.

"Show off," Efram says, his voice neutral. "Now let's go."

As I follow them towards their quarters, I look between the three men, reaching out with my energy, trying to sense any jealousy. I don't pick up any, at all. How can that be? I know Silas wants me, Efram and I have had more than one 'moment,' and now Rafe just shoved his tongue in my mouth, and the other two are okay with it?

My mind spins with possibilities. Stupid girl, get a grip. Sooner or later I'll have to choose, of that I have no doubt. Until that time there's no point in worrying.

The room the guys are sharing is about the size of the bathroom in my room. I'm not surprised, and in truth it's a nice room. Nicer than what I grew up in, and nicer than what I stayed in way back in Bunker E247.

Rafe rushes over to what must be his bunk, looks around with a devious grin, then digs under the mattress and pulls out a dark bottle.

"Voila!" he exclaims, holding it up triumphantly.

"Only you," Efram says, shaking his head.

"I do have a very particular skill set," Rafe grins.

Rafe scrounges up glasses and pours drinks. Standing in a circle, our energies flowing in and around each other, a strange sensation comes over me. Contentment. Everything is as it should be, here, in this circle, with these men. We belong together. Odd though it may be, for this one moment I feel like everything is going to be okay. If only it would last, because I know it won't, but I'll take it while I've got it.

CHAPTER TWENTY-EIGHT

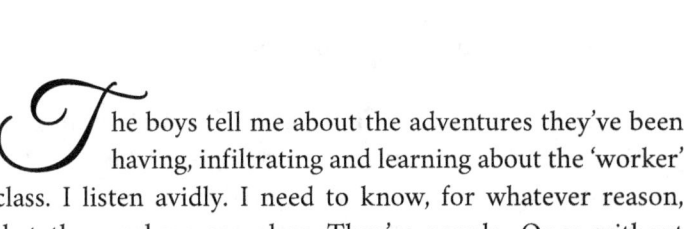

*T*he boys tell me about the adventures they've been having, infiltrating and learning about the 'worker' class. I listen avidly. I need to know, for whatever reason, that the workers are okay. They're people. Ones without options. I've seen how the disenfranchised are treated in Bunker Society. If we're going to be here awhile, I need to know they're at least getting a fair shake of it.

Besides, with all the vanity and backstabbing I've picked up on in the upper levels, these people sound like they're much more my speed. Down to earth, normal. Listening to each of the guys talk is soothing on my nerves too. I love listening to their voices. It's music to my ears.

"I came across a Coven," Nathaniel says, partway through narrating his exploits.

Something thrums inside of me, and I sit up straighter. It doesn't go unnoticed.

"Aviella?" Rafe asks.

"A Coven?" I ask.

When I say the word, I feel a buzz deep inside myself again. There's something about this.

"Yes," Nathaniel says, his eyes unreadable.

Biting my lower lip, I try to put my finger on what it is. No one says anything, obviously waiting for me. It's like an annoying mosquito buzzing in my ear.

"Aviella?" Efram asks.

"There's something about this," I say, vocalizing my thought. "I don't know what it is, but I feel like we should talk to them."

"Are you sure that's wise?" Silas says. "It doesn't sound like something Tynan is going to be a fan of, having witches in his lower levels. We do not want to stir the Dragon's ire."

"Surely you can handle him," Rafe says, poking at the Methuselah.

"My ability to handle or not handle Tynan is not in question," Silas says. "My willingness to risk his upset over something when we don't have to is the question at hand."

"I think it's important," I say. I don't have time for the boys to argue.

"Then that's what we'll do," Efram says.

I smile, grateful for his support. The others nod their assent. After a brief discussion, we decide to go after we have a meal. The food here is simple, more in line with what I'm used to, but good. Good old Nutrimeal, standby of the Apocalypse.

The conversation during dinner is muted. I can't take my thoughts away from this Coven. There's something important about it. At last we're ready. Nathaniel leads the way to where he saw the witches. Our ragtag group attracts a lot of attention as we move through the passages. Sidelong glances and people rushing to get out of our way while trying to appear like they aren't in a hurry. I don't blame them. If I weren't part of this group, I'd probably be afraid too. It's the only sensible response in the Apocalypse.

"I first sensed them here," Nathaniel says, gesturing with his hand.

I close my eyes, and focus my awareness. It's more than my normal senses, I use my magic, reaching out with my energy. I think it works like the laws of attraction, like calling to like. I don't actually know, I'm no scholar, but it's my own working theory. I should discuss this with Silas at some point. I'm sure he has theories of his own.

When I expand my awareness, there is a tingle to my left. The tingle becomes an itch as I move in that direction, which I take to be a good sign. When I open my eyes and look around, we've moved quite a distance.

"Do you guys feel that?" I ask.

"Yes," Nathaniel answers first.

The others nod. Good, I'm on the right path. Taking the lead, I head down one hall and then another, following my instincts. When I turn a corner, a young man is standing in the middle of the hallway with his arms crossed over his chest and a glower on his face.

"What you be wanting?" he asks, his voice heavy with an accent I don't recognize.

"We come looking for friends," I say, smiling.

"You be coming to the wrong place," he says, shaking his head negative. "No friends be found here. You not welcome."

"Well, how about if I came looking for other people who are special?"

"People who be special, they be upstairs," he says, doubt showing in his eyes.

This isn't going anywhere fast, so I decide to short-circuit it. Closing my eyes, I reach out with my magic, envisioning a soft, white light. Suddenly the world beyond my closed eyes flashes. I open my eyes and butterflies turn in my stomach, I'm shocked by what I see.

The young man in front of me is covering his eyes with

his hands, tears streaming out from under them. Rafe is laughing loudly, so hard tears are flowing from his eyes also. Efram and Silas are rubbing their eyes and blinking rapidly. Nathaniel looks at me, frowning. I smile, sheepishly, and shrug.

"Oh, that is classic," Rafe says. "I'm gonna rank that one just below the making of wine."

"You're a jerk," I say, halfheartedly punching him in the arm.

It only makes him laugh harder. Ass.

"What be wrong with you?" the young man exclaims. "No display, them's the rules. You be attracting attention."

"Sorry," I say, as he lowers his hands from his eyes, still blinking rapidly. "Sometimes it gets out of control."

"You be like us," he says. "Come with me."

He turns and walks away. I follow without hesitation. A couple of turns later and we're outside a door on which he knocks. A muffled voice says something, and he turns the handle, pushing the door open. He doesn't enter himself, stepping to one side, motioning for us to go in.

It's not really a bunk that we go into, but something that was probably once a meeting space. It's empty with a concrete floor and corrugated steel walls. A group of men and women stand in a loose circle as if they are waiting for us.

The break in the circle is at the door we entered, firmly placing us in the center of all of them. I hope this isn't a trap. If it is, they're going to regret it. We're a nuclear option. Looking around the circle, I make a quick count. There are eighteen of them, ten men, eight women. The aura in the room is serious, but not dangerous. They stand with their hands in front of them, fingers curled and touching, forming an upside-down heart before each of them. They all have a glowing mark that looks like it's tattooed between the thumb and forefinger. The way they are holding their hands makes it a complete rune of a coiled snake.

"How long have you all been part of the Snake Coven?" Nathaniel asks.

"We were born into it," a tall, stately woman answers.

She has her hair pulled back into a tight bun. She has stormy gray eyes and what would be commonly known as resting bitch face.

Nathaniel nods as if all of this mean something to him. I can feel the magic. It's not overly powerful, but it is strong. There's something more, though. A familiar signature that tugs at my memory. Nathaniel talks with the woman for a few moments, discussing the details of their Coven. While they talk I focus on the energy.

Suddenly it hits me. It's the same feeling I felt around the Innocents. There is a Chosen One here, somewhere. I try to trace it down but it's faint, a hint of the power that is to come. I guess that makes sense, if they were full-blown then the Mages would already be here, ready to collect them.

"The Prophecy is clear," the woman is saying to Nathaniel.

"You have to be careful with prophecy," Efram says. "It's always open to interpretation."

"It is clear," she repeats, firmly.

Efram nods and doesn't say more.

"What prophecy?" I ask.

"When the Beast comes to feed, we will inherit the Bunker above," she says, a low murmur of assent or blessing comes from those circled around us.

Cold chills run down my arms. When the Beast feeds, and they think that's a good thing? I suppress a shudder. Anger pulses from them, hitting me in a flurry, pounding against my senses. It's difficult to not be left reeling by the vehemence of their emotions.

"Sounds… chilling," I say.

She turns her stormy eyes on me, frowning deeper, somehow. I smile in response, hoping to break through or annoy her or something.

"You do not understand," she says, shaking her head.

"No, sorry," I shrug.

I don't understand, and I am sorry. They don't seem to have it that bad. We've seen much worse by far, hello Wormwood Bunker as a prime example. This place is virtually heaven compared to that place. I wish I understood why they're so upset though.

She resumes her conversation. Nathaniel seems to be the only person she's actually willing to talk to. The only thing that comes clear to me in their discussion is their blind faith and following of this "prophecy."

"We should be more hospitable," she says.

She nods towards one of the young men, and he steps forward out of the circle.

"I will prepare a meal," he says. "If you would care to join us."

I exchange a glance with Rafe and Efram and Silas, almost as one we shrug. It's not like we have anything better to do.

"That would be very nice," I say.

He smiles and leads us towards a door at the back of the room. The other side of it is set up like a regular dining hall. Long tables with benches line the room. Several of the Coven members tag along with us. They all set to work, and it isn't long before food is placed before us.

The atmosphere has become friendlier. The tension drops away in the face of food and general comradeship. I enjoy visiting with them. Listening to their stories, whether or not focused on their prophecy and their underlying anger, it becomes clear that their life here isn't really bad.

They may not have a lot of choices, but who does? The

Apocalypse has happened. Survival, for most, is in question every day. This place is far from the worst. It's better than Bunker E247 was, and one hell of a sight better than Wormwood Bunker. One way or another, they're surviving and they have regular routines.

I scan around the room hoping to spot the Innocents. There are a couple that feel slightly different but it's not the same. What does become clear to me is they have power, a lot of it when they're combined. This whole thing is a powder keg that could possibly go off at any time. I wonder if Tynan knows about it. I can't imagine he doesn't.

Efram seems at home here. They crowd around him, pestering him with questions, and sharing stories. He fairly glows being the center of attention. I'm happy for him. He seems to be in his element.

One of the men sits down across from me. He has a scar that runs along his right cheek from his ear to the corner of his mouth. It gives him a permanent grimace. He stares at me for a long moment in silence.

"You're just the sort of woman they look to corrupt when they have their parties," he says.

"Excuse me?" I ask.

He chews a mouthful of food slowly, staring at me. At last he swallows it, shakes his head, takes a drink and then finally answers.

"They will try to corrupt you," he says. "It's what they do."

"And you are?"

"Merric," he replies.

"Okay, Merric, what do you mean?"

"The Darlings," he says, somewhat cryptically.

"What about them?"

"Don't you get it?" he sighs, setting his fork down. "It's all a sham. A show put on for their entertainment. You would be a perfect fit for it."

"I'm no one's entertainment," I say, anger flaring.

"Good, don't let them use you," he says, picking up his tray and walking away.

The conversation with Merric leaves a bad taste in my mouth. I'm ready to go home. I catch Rafe's eye and make a motion with my head. He picks up on it, like I hoped he would, and taps Nathaniel on the shoulder. In just a few moments we're taking our leave.

"That was fun," I quip on our way back to the boys' rooms.

"I do love a side of fanatic with my dinner," Rafe says.

"They're not that bad," Efram says, coming to their defense.

"Uh-huh," I say, half-teasing. "Says the life of the party."

"I wasn't—" he objects.

"Right. Oh Efram, is your dinner warm enough? Here, let me heat that some more for you," I tease.

Efram blushes brightly, and I can't hold back my laughter.

"It wasn't that bad, was it?" he asks.

"No," I assure him. "It was much, much worse."

"I'm not going to live this down anytime soon am I?" he asks.

"Most assuredly not," Rafe says.

"They did seem overly fond of you," Silas says.

"Great," Efram shakes his head.

We enter the guys' room and then we're all standing around looking at each other. I'm feeling awkward. I have to go, and I know it, but I don't want to. I want to stay here, with them, where I belong. I want... well let's not go there. Brain, stop the images now, thank you very much.

"Aviella, I need to tell you something," Nathaniel says.

He feels heavy. Dread hits me out of nowhere. I'm not going to like where this is going.

"Yeah?" I ask, giving him a sidelong look.

"I have to leave, for a while," he says.

A bomb couldn't affect me more. Staring at him in stunned silence, my mouth hanging open and my eyes wide, I try to process his words.

"You... can't," I say at last.

Good job, Aviella, great argument, well-articulated. I'm sure that will change his mind.

"I have to," he says.

"Yeah, on that note—" Rafe says.

"No, not you too," I say, voice cracking.

"I have duties," Nathaniel says. "Another trumpet has sounded. I have matters that I must attend."

"But," I say.

There's nothing to say. Rafe and Nathaniel look sad but determined. I don't own them, I can't control them, and it's clear they've made up their minds. The emptiness feels like a black hole. My stomach drops, and I'm left reeling.

"We're going to make sure you're safe first," Rafe says. "The world out there is changing, again. I have contacts that will swarm to the chaos. They'll have information we can use."

"Both of you?" I ask, feeling desperate.

They glance at each other, and Nathaniel shrugs.

"I didn't plan this," Nathaniel says, as if that makes any of it better.

"Right," I say. "Got it."

Damn. Every time I feel like I've got things coming to a place where I can be happy, someone leaves, or I lose them. Is this the real story of my life? How many people can Aviella lose before she goes over the edge? Numb and fighting tears, we exchange hugs, and I leave for my room.

CHAPTER TWENTY-NINE

The room is too big, too empty.

I know it's not any different than it was before I went to the lower levels, logically, but it feels different now. Rafe and Nathaniel are gone, or as good as. They're leaving tonight.

What if something happens to them? I'll never know. They'll just be gone, forever. Lost, unknown. Magical energy races up and down my limbs, making the hairs on my arms stand on end. Pacing to the wall and back again, I struggle against the urge to punch the wall. I'd probably hurt myself, and what good would that do anyone?

I hate losing people.

Hate it. Hate, hate, hate it.

Ever since Dad. Tears well up, and anger rises right behind them. Damn it, I'm not going to cry! My throat locks up, and my chest tightens as I struggle with the overwhelm of emotions. Pacing faster, maybe I can outrun it. Of course I can't.

Someone knocks on the door.

"Great," I choke.

Glancing at myself in the mirror, I can't stand what I see. My eyes are puffy, tears sitting in the corners, and I look washed out. Perfect, who could possibly be at my door right now?

Taking a deep breath, I make them wait. They knock again but at least I'm able to get the tears under control. Nothing I can do about my puffy eyes, but screw it. I don't want company anyway. I storm to the door and throw it open.

"What!" I bark.

The staffer who showed me to my room jumps at my harsh tone, making me feel bad. It's not her fault. I should be nice.

She's holding a small, flat, white box that she almost drops. She fumbles to keep ahold of it while also trying to back away from me.

"Sorry," I say, reaching out and catching the box before it hits the floor.

It's surprisingly light. She looks from the box in my hands up to me then back again, biting her lower lip. She motions at the box with a half-gesture, then shakes her head.

"Uh," she mumbles. "Lord Tynan invites you to uh —the—uh…"

"It's fine," I say. "What's your name? I don't think I caught it last time."

She looks at my eyes and blushes cherry pink.

"Uh—Sam," she says, nodding for emphasis. "Samantha, but everyone, I mean you can, uh—call me Sam."

"Okay, Sam. Thank you, I'm Aviella," I extend a hand.

She stares at it wide-eyed, then tentatively takes it. She's regaining her composure, standing straighter, and trying on a smile.

"I'm sorry," she offers.

"Not your fault," I say. "Now, why were you here?"

She looks at the box in my hand, frowning. She reaches, so I hand it back to her. She breathes a sigh of relief.

"Lord Tynan requests your company for this evening's contest," she says.

Her smile grows broader as she opens the box, holding it between us. Inside is a stunning emerald necklace. It catches the light, sparkling brightly. It takes my breath away.

"He likes you," she adds, obviously feeling it's a good thing to have his attention.

Except I'd rather not. He's a Dragon, and the way he makes me feel... I'm not sure I can control myself around him, or what the implications would be if I don't. Also, this necklace—is he trying to buy me? Well, I'm not for sale, I don't care who or what you are.

I stare at the necklace for too long. Her hand trembles, pulling me out of my thoughts. Looking up, I nod, unable to think of anything nice to say in response. She's not going to understand. In her mind, having Tynans's attention would be the greatest thing that could possibly happen to her.

"Thank you," I say, unable to find anything more appropriate.

"He asked I help you select what to wear," she adds. "Since you're new here and all. He wants you to feel at home."

Oh, I'm sure he does, all right. Closing my eyes, I count to five, then open them.

"Sure," I say, unwilling to take my emotions out on her. She's innocent in all of this.

Stepping to the side, I let her in. She makes her way straight to the armoire and pulls out clothes. Great, here I go, what am I getting into now?

I PULL THE DRESS DOWN FOR THE UMPTEEN-MILLIONTH TIME.

It rides up something fierce. Still, I look good. Checking myself out in the mirror, I turn from one side to the other and admire myself. The dress is a slinky red number, strapless again, but it really makes me look better than I ever thought I could. I thought the last one was stunning, but this takes it to an entirely new level.

Sam wanted me to wear heels, but no way I'm down with that. Instead we settled on some sensible flats that still look nice. I know, heels are the rage, but I can count the number of 'affairs' like this I've gone to on one hand, and almost all of them have ended with me running. No way I'm wearing heels. It is the Apocalypse after all.

Satisfied, I turn one last time, and there's a knock on the door.

"Wow," Silas says, his eyes drinking me in.

My heart rate speeds up in an instant as my body responds to him. His energy surrounds me, caressing, holding me, and I want, very much, for him to take me in his arms. Swallowing hard, I force a smile.

"You like?" I ask, butterflies dancing in my stomach.

"Like?" he says, shaking his head. "That is an entirely insufficient word…"

"Yeah?" I ask, feeling like a little girl needing his approval. God, what is wrong with me?

He nods, and his tongue darts out, wetting his lips. He swallows, not taking his eyes off me. The final verdict doesn't come from his words, but when I notice the front of his slacks swelling. Smiling, I nod, satisfied that I look as good as I thought.

"We should go," he says, his voice low, soft, and sensual.

"Right," I say.

He holds out a hand and I take it, linking arms with him. We walk to the event in silence. Lots of people are out in the halls, all of them dressed to perfection. I draw a lot of attention, both male and female. It's impossible to ignore the whisper campaign I leave in my wake. A lot of folks are not happy with me.

Whatever, I don't care for them either. I don't think anyone should live in luxury if it comes on the backs of others. It's not right. Everyone should have to work and contribute, not just those unfortunate enough to be born to the wrong family.

They're nothing more than a bunch of half-starved, over-competitive bunch of dilettantes who bring nothing of value besides their looks. None of them would know a decent day's work if it bit them on the butt.

Music is thumping, growing louder as the crowd increases. Soon it's a veritable throng around us, and we slow as the crowd becomes a line.

"What is this?" I ask Silas, rising on my toes to speak into his ear so he can hear me.

"A fashion show, mostly," he says.

"Oh," I say. "Do you think—"

I'm cut off as two burly men push through the crowd and stop in front of us. Magic rises and my skin itches as my power almost bursts out on its own. That hasn't happened like that in a long time. The boys have really worked with me to help me stay in control, but when I'm startled it's harder.

I cut it off before anything happens, but it takes an effort. Silas's hand tightens on my arm, and I know he felt it too.

"What is this?" Silas asks.

"Lord Tynan sent us to escort her to the VIP room," one of them says.

"Oh," I say, blushing.

"Very well," Silas says, stepping out of line and taking me with him.

"Just her," the other one says.

"What? No!" I exclaim.

"I'm sure Tynan won't object to my joining him," Silas says.

His words resonate when he says them. I don't hear them with my ears alone, but through my energy, they carry magic. The two men exchange a look, then shrug.

"Of course," one of them says.

They lead us out of the crowd, which of course creates even more whispers. Feeling impulsive, I look over my shoulder at the crowd, all of whom are watching, openly or not, and give a finger wave. A couple of the women gasp, which is perfect.

"Having fun?" Silas asks.

"Yes. Yes, I am," I say, feeling self-satisfied.

"Aviella," Tynan greets me, rising to his feet as we enter the room.

"Tynan," I say, smiling when he notices Silas and seeing something in his face shift.

"Silas," Tynan says to him.

"A pleasure to see you again," Silas says, ignoring the tension in Tynan.

"Well, the show is about to begin. Let's take our seats," Tynan says.

He leads the way across the small room. We're on a balcony that overlooks the crowd below. There's a runway that extends down the middle of the room. The seats around the space are filling up fast.

The music is pounding louder, increasing in volume until it crescendos in one final loud blast and stops suddenly. The crowd bursts into applause. A man with bright blue hair spiked up off the top of his head walks through the curtain and down the runway. He turns slowly, looking the crowd over, then raises the microphone to his mouth.

"Ladies and gentlemen," he says, his voice echoing. "Are you ready?"

The crowd cheers and applauds. I glance at Tynan. He appears bored, resting his chin in his hand and tapping a finger on his cheek. He's barely paying attention. He notices me watching and smiles.

"You look quite lovely tonight," he says.

"Thank you," I say. "An admirer sent me this necklace."

His smile broadens. Suddenly I feel like putty in his hands, like a melting chocolate bar ready to be consumed. Involuntarily I lean in closer to him. Desire thrums through me. His eyes are dark pools, his lips full and inviting. There's a fire burning in me, rising higher, if it keeps going it's going to consume me. I'm not sure if I care.

The crowd cheers louder, breaking the moment. I turn away from him, and I'm panting. It's too hot, I'm about to break out in a sweat. Focusing on the event below, I struggle to ignore him and the effect he is having.

Rail-thin girls parade down the walkway in dresses that are even more revealing than the one I have on. They sway their hips, pout their lips, doing everything they can to be deemed worthy.

Watching this display breaks the spell Tynan has on me. These women are displaying themselves in this disgusting show in the hopes that they will be chosen to be a "Darling." The cutthroat nature of this competition is obvious. Food is scarce in the Apocalypse, but nowhere else have I seen girls so thin, almost to the point of being gaunt. I don't know why, but it is obviously the standard of beauty here in Bunker 3. I've seen it among all the well-to-do.

The last of the girls marches out and down the runway and then joins the others standing in front of the curtain. They're trying to show themselves to best effect. The announcer steps back out on the runway and walks to the end.

"Ladies and gentlemen there you have it. The competitors

have shown you their stuff, and now it's up to you, who will you put through? Remember, only the most beautiful can be welcomed into our ranks. Anyone less would not be worthy of being a Darling."

A soft murmur runs through the crowd as they mark their votes on tally sheets. Drab gray-clad workers make their way through the crowd gathering the sheets. The entire display is disgusting. I glance over at Tynan. He's watching me, not the show.

"Happy?" I ask, arching an eyebrow.

"Always," he says with an enigmatic smile.

Desire wars with outrage, and I'm not sure which one is going to win. Silas sits on the other side of Tynan quietly watching. He makes no move to intervene or add to the conversation.

"You know this is wrong, right?" I ask.

"By whose standard?" Tynan asks.

"Anyone who is sane?" I respond, and he laughs, loud.

"The votes are in," the announcer says, his voice covering over Tynan's laughter.

I look down at the show. Several guards have appeared on the stage standing behind the line of candidates. The announcer strolls along the walkway with a ridiculous swagger. He makes his way to the end of the line of girls.

He looks the first girl up and down, a fixed smile on his face. The crowd chants, it's too soft for me to make out the words. The announcer walks past the first girl to stop in front of the second. He shakes his head side to side.

"Sorry," he says smiling.

A guard grabs that girl and pulls her off the stage. I'm on my feet in an instant, magic surging, as the crowd explodes with applause and cheers.

"No!" I say.

"Aviella!" Silas says.

I whirl on my heel and confront Tynan.

"You can't let this be!" I say.

"Can't I?" Tynan asks, an easy smile on his face.

"No, it isn't right," I say, righteously indignant.

Those girls have put themselves through hell to get here. They don't deserve to be treated like this. No human should be fodder for the amusement of a crowd. It's not right.

"They make their choices. No one forces them to do this," Tynan says.

"Sure they do! What choices do they have?" I retort, thrumming with anger which is burning out any hint of desire.

Tynan smiles. "This is life in the Apocalypse. I do not create it or encourage it. This is what they've made for themselves. It is their game, not mine."

Something about his words stun me to silence. What am I supposed to say to that? They created it, not him?

The truth in his words is undeniable. They ring through me, and in some way, I see what he's saying. I was a kid when the Apocalypse started, but I saw a lot in my early years. Dad kept us on the move. He was prepared when the Apocalypse came. He always said Mom made sure he was on his path. He wanted me to see the world as it was and made sure I met all kinds of people. Then the Orphanage was full of cliques, none of which I belonged in. I was always the outsider.

The world before the Apocalypse was full of classes, the haves and the have-nots. Could it be that is the way we create the world? Is that what I'm fighting to save?

No. I'm not trying to save the world, I want to create a new one. A balanced world. A world that is fair, damn it.

Unable and unwilling to argue with him further, I plop back into my seat and wait out the rest of the show in sullen silence, hating everything because I can't argue with him.

As the display comes to an end, Tynan rises. I follow his

lead as does Silas, and we walk out of the area. When I step through the door, I feel the air around me change. It becomes electric, alive with power that almost crackles with intensity.

"Brother," Alaric says to Tynan.

Alaric and Shen, Tynan's brothers and two more of the Horsemen of the Apocalypse. My stomach sinks. Great.

CHAPTER THIRTY

*A*laric and Shen scan me, their energy passing over in waves. It's a heady feeling, like being drunk. It makes me light-headed and spinning. It's an effort of will to not stumble backwards.

"Brothers," Tynan smiles.

Swallowing hard, I struggle to maintain some semblance of composure. Every nerve in my body feels alive, burning with need and desire. Their attention is a drug that leaves me quivering, craving more. My skin tingles under their attention.

"We thought we'd join you... for the show," Shen says, his eyes never leaving me.

"An excellent idea," Tynan says. "Will you join us?"

Tynan gestures towards a hall to one side, and his eyes are on me. All their eyes are, like they can't get enough of me. It's strangely empowering and yet disconcerting. It's a long moment before I realize his question was for me. Flushing with embarrassment, I scramble for an answer, having completely lost my train of thought.

"Oh, uh, yeah," I say, nodding.

Only after I say it do I think of Silas, but when I turn to catch his eye, he's nowhere to be seen. Thanks Silas, way to be my hero. He was the one control factor I knew I could count on in this situation. I know, with the absolute certainty of the hormones raging in my body already, that my judgment is going to be crap.

Tynan leads the way and Shen and Alaric flank me. Their energy caresses me as we walk, twisting and combining with mine. It's the strangest, most erotic, daring walk I've ever taken. Outside nothing is happening. Four people walking down a hallway, but on another level it's a different story.

Every nerve tingles. I'm hyper-sensitive. The feel of the air we're walking through almost sends me into an overload. None of us say a word—they're unnecessary. Extraneous. I'm the center of their attention, and yet not one of them is looking at me, with their eyes anyway.

Licking my lips, I try to work moisture back into my mouth, as I believe it is being drawn to one singular point of my body. Am I doing this?

Images flash through my thoughts in a blur, so fast I'm not sure what they are. My heart pounds and I'm breathing in short, quick bursts.

Tynan opens a door and stands to one side, letting me walk in first. I half-expect to walk into a bedroom, and I'm not sure I'd turn away if I did, but fortunately that decision isn't the one I face.

It's a sitting room, with three couches, two love seats, and four chairs arranged strategically to face each other. A massive fireplace on the right wall has a bright, crackling fire burning cheerily in it. The far wall across from us is floor-to-ceiling windows looking out over the lake and its gorgeous views. It's nighttime outside, but the moon is mostly full, casting soft silvery light that shimmers across the surface of the water.

I walk to the window and stare out. It's a breathtaking view, but more than that it gives me a moment to collect my thoughts and try to get my body under control. I've been riding on the edge for a long time now. There's been no release for the deep, aching need of my body since all this started. It's the worst possible time for me to be thrown into this situation.

A hand touches my lower back and I jump, fire racing across my skin from even that simple contact. Tynan is on my right, staring out the window too. Alaric steps up on my left, and then his hand rests on my back just above his brother's. Shen stands behind me, so close I sense his body, but he's not touching me, not quite.

I can't catch my breath. My head spins as my heart pounds harder. This isn't me. I'm not the girl anyone wants, least of all three men who are this incredibly sexy. They're the Horsemen! What am I thinking? What am I doing?

No one says a word, standing in silence that over the span of time becomes comfortable. They don't move, they don't talk, and then it hits me. I'm in control. They're letting me have the lead, not pushing their agenda, but offering themselves to me. Blood rushes to my head making me sway.

The hands on my back increase their pressure, steadying me. Turning my head towards Tynan, my lips parting, words fail me when I see the desire in his eyes burning like a beacon in the night. He moves in, and his lips claim mine.

Moaning, I return the kiss, giving myself over. Hands touch the bare skin of my shoulders, causing a thrill to run through me at the first contact of skin to skin.

Alaric kisses his way from my shoulder down my right arm. Shen presses himself against my backside. His manhood digs in against my ass, impressing me with its size and stiffness.

Tynan's tongue presses against my lips, tasting me, then

in a rush, he drives it past that fleshy barrier. It enters my mouth as a raging invader, claiming all that lies before it. My tongue battles with his, fighting his claim.

Shen's hands are on my ass, squeezing, stroking, and rubbing. Alaric's tongue traces delightful lines around the bare skin of my arm while his hands stroke my thigh, moving higher and closer, but stopping before he reaches my core.

Tynan pushes forward, forcing me harder against Shen. I'm sandwiched between them, their raging hard cocks digging into me, pronouncing their desire and dominance. But they're not dominant. I am. I'm the center, I'm in control, and I know it.

Alaric kisses lower, across my forearm and down, lowering himself to his knees next to me. His hand roams up my legs, and at last comes to rest cupping my mound. I groan as he applies pressure, pulling up. He makes a circular motion, eliciting another groan.

Tynan grabs my lower lip between his teeth, gently tugging as he nibbles. Darting my tongue out, I taste his lips which are sweet and musky at the same time. It's distinctly manly. A heady combination.

My dress slides higher until cool air is on my ass. Shen slides my panties down so his caresses are now on bare skin. His cock presses hard between the cheeks of my ass, so I grind back against it while Alaric rubs harder on my mound, applying pressure to my clit.

Pleasure courses through my veins.

I've danced on the edge of release for so long, unable to get relief, and I can't hold back. Can't stop this.

Their kisses cover my body. Hands, six of them, cover my body, touching me everywhere. My heart races, breath is ragged, an orgasm builds.

My dirtiest fantasies, the most wrong thoughts I've ever entertained, are coming true.

Three incredibly sexy, perfect men focusing all their attention on me.

I'm the center of their need and it is need, more than lust. Their energy, twisting in and out of mine as soon their bodies will enter mine, tells me the truth.

They need me. Together we'll make a whole.

Tynan grips the top of my dress, and in a single motion he slides it down, exposing my breasts.

Cool air hits my nipples, and I gasp, but Alaric places his mouth over the right, and Shen reaches around, covering the left with his hand.

The three of them press against me, encapsulating me from three sides. Leaning my head back, I rest it on Shen's shoulder, breaking my lips away from Tynan. Shen's lips seek mine, pressing against them.

I drive my tongue past his full, hard lips, seeking his tongue. He catches it lightly with his teeth, nibbling. Sensation is carrying me away.

Hands, touches, kisses, everywhere.

A hand, I don't know whose, slides up my right thigh, while another hand continues to rub me.

The hand up my thigh touches my stomach, and it quivers at the touch.

Fingers slide under my panties, passive over my mound, pushing the hand already there aside.

Parting my lower lips, exposing my wetness for the first time, it explores my secret folds. Groaning I thrust my hips forward, driving it in deeper, wanting to fill the aching emptiness.

Everything flashes white.

"AVIELLA!" Dad's voice echoes, calling to me.

The room is gone, replaced by silvery white light. He's in pain. I feel it deep in my bones.

"Dad?" I call, my voice quavering.

I turn and the silver-white shimmers. Outlines of images almost form, shapes that I almost recognize before the strange symbols I don't understand replace them.

Ghostly apparitions surround me. Suddenly I realize they're the Dragons, or the outlines of them, here with me. Where ever here is.

"Avi..." his voice is cut off.

I run towards it, sort of. There is no here, there is no there, exactly, but as I move, the light shifts and changes as if I'm moving past things.

Ahead I spot a darkness, so I head towards that.

"Dad!" I yell.

"Aviella," he says, his voice tight and high.

The sounds of cracking whips break the air, then there is a sizzling sound and the scent of burning flesh fills my senses.

"NO!" I scream.

Images flash fast before me, and for an instant he's right in front of me. He's on a rack over an open fire being burned alive. His skin is peeling back, his mouth open in a scream, demons look on, laughing, as they turn him on a spit.

It's gone as fast as it comes.

Silver-white surrounds me, and a calmness comes with it. A brighter light forms, shimmering and coming closer. Peace comes with it, a certainty and calmness that makes no sense.

"Save him, Aviella," a soft, womanly voice says.

An ache forms in my chest, and sadness causes tears to well in my eyes. I know that voice.

"Mom?" I ask, choking on tears.

"Save him," the voice says but now it's like it's coming from a long distance away, down a tunnel, barely there. A whisper on the wind.

. . .

"How?" I sob, knees refusing to hold me up, I drop.

Tynan catches me, sweeping me off my feet and carrying me to a couch. As he lays me down, Shen covers me with a blanket, giving me back a sense of modesty.

The mood between us is broken, and they know it, for which I'm thankful. Looking at the three Dragons circling me, my cheeks burn hot.

"I'm sorry," I say, unable to meet their eyes.

The three of them look at each other before Tynan speaks.

"We saw it," he says. "With you."

My heart stops. Can't get a breath in. Time doesn't move. Staring into Tynan's eyes now, I scan him and feel the truth in his words. They saw my vision, with me.

That's never happened. That can't happen. Yet it did.

Swallowing, I blink rapidly as time resumes and my heart finds its rhythm again.

"Seriously?" I ask, still doubting.

The three men nod, their faces grave.

What does this mean? It changes everything, doesn't it? If they saw it, then that has to mean they're connected.

Whatever it is I'm facing, God knows I need allies. Three of the four Horsemen, Dragons to boot, would be very powerful allies to have.

"We will help you find your father," Tynan says.

The universe clicks when he speaks, and something shifts. Something so fundamental, so central, that it makes me feel like everything has changed. It's nothing I can point to or put into words. It's a feeling. A strange, wonderful feeling, and I'm certain I've taken the next step on my path.

Fate's hand. That's the feeling. Fate has moved a piece on the board, and it's shifted the game.

Weird. Taking a deep breath, I let it out slowly and nod. Rising to a sitting position, I do my best to right my clothing under the blanket. Strange, a moment ago I was all ready and couldn't care less how much of me they saw—I wanted them to see me—but now I'm demure.

Don't think about it. There's no time for carnal thoughts and pleasures. My dad is in trouble. I must save him. It's on me.

Sliding my dress back into place over my chest, I look at the three of them. I don't know what to do next. An awkward and uncomfortable feeling settles on me as I struggle to meet each of their eyes. Their gazes are intense. Apparently, they have no problem switching gears from sex to action. Unfortunately, I don't have this skill.

"Thank you," I say, finally, unable to find better words.

Tynan smiles and a tingle runs down my spine. My God, how can he be interested in me? He's so damn sexy, it's stunning how good-looking he is. Blinking, I push those thoughts aside.

"We need to make a plan," Tynan says. "Those symbols, I'm not familiar with them."

"I have some thoughts," Alaric says, moving to sit beside me on the couch.

He touches my shoulder with his fingertips, tracing idle patterns on my skin.

"We have some texts we could consult," Shen says, taking my other side and doing the same.

A shudder racks my body, I try to suppress it, but I can't. Their touch is too... enticing.

"Brothers," Tynan says, soft but commanding.

The two Dragons look at him and something passes between all of them. It's not words or anything I understand exactly, but instinctively I know, feeling it in their energies.

Alaric and Shen take their hands off me and the air around us changes. The sexual desire is gone as fast and as easy as if they flipped a light switch. I gasp in surprise, left with an empty feeling where it was.

"There is much to do," Alaric says. "We should go, Shen."

"Right," Shen says, rising to his feet.

Shen turns towards me, and takes my hand in his. Slowly he raises it to his lips, his eyes locked on mine, his lips soft and wet as he kisses my hand then gently places it back in my lap. My heart skips a beat, and desire sends out one lone flare.

Alaric does the same, though his lips are fuller and drier, creating an entirely different sensation. The two of them walk away without another word, leaving Tynan and me alone.

We stare at each other across the short distance between the couch I'm on and the chair he's in. His eyes dance with delight. Our energies meld in the silence, and I probe at him with mine. Suddenly he opens himself to me, inviting me in.

It's the first time I've felt him fully as himself. Ancient beyond words, strong, certain, and yet bored and plagued by his own doubts. Seeing beyond the exterior, I find the person behind the front, and a bond forms between the two of us, because in seeing him he sees me as I am too.

He sees my revulsion at the classist system of the Bunkers, but as he does I see his indifference to it. I understand it truly isn't something he or the other Dragons created, but what man does to man. It doesn't stem from them, but they don't do anything to right it. My concern with it is a new thought to this ancient creature and flies in the face of his general disdain.

"Aviella," Tynan says, pulling back from the connection between us, but the line remains, albeit partially closed.

"Tynan," I say, staring into his eyes.

I'm seeing him in a new light than before. Things will never be the same.

CHAPTER THIRTY-ONE

TYNAN

*S*lamming my walls back in place, I try to shut her out but only partially succeed. She's powerful, more powerful than anything I've encountered in a very long time.

My brothers and I have fought and hunted across the ages, and never has any creature been so vexing and fascinating at the same time. She doesn't know it, that much is obvious. She has no idea her true potential.

She is intoxicating. A heady drink that must be savored, taken slowly for too much too fast could be the end of me. I'm caught in her gravity and I know it. Nothing will ever be the same again. It can't be. She has changed it all.

My decision is made, for better or worse, we will help her. The Horsemen aiding a mortal girl. I never would have thought it but in her, maybe I can find purpose once again. My role in this world was over. Having a reason, any reason, is better than how we've been living.

I feel the shift in the universe as I make the decision.

"You should rest," I say.

Aviella nods, biting her lower lip. My cock stirs, but now is not the time for such pleasures as her flesh will give. There is work to be done, and that must come first.

"I'll have you escorted to your quarters," I say, closing the door on my desire for now.

CHAPTER THIRTY-TWO

"I don't care, it all sucks," I say, shoving the last of my meager possessions into my backpack.

"I know," Efram says. "I don't like it either."

Looking up, I glare then shake my head and plop down on the bed. Efram sits next to me, his hands in his lap, keeping a small space between us. That space might as well be a million miles. Everything is changing, again.

"I hate change," I pout.

I've earned it; this sucks. I also hate pouting, but damn it when can I catch a break? Rafe and Nathaniel gone, now Silas wants me to go with him and the Dragons, but Efram has to remain here. Ugh, this is terrible.

"I know," he says, his hand moving towards my leg, but then he pulls it back without touching me.

What the hell, Efram? Why the distance?

"Out with it," I say, twisting around so I'm facing him.

"What?" he asks, looking confused, but I see past that mask.

He knows what I'm talking about. Instead of answering

him, I stare him down. He looks away first, and I smile. Point for me.

"Say it," I demand.

"I..." he stops, staring at the floor and obviously searching for the words. I understand that, so I wait him out, letting him figure it out. "I don't know where we... stand."

"What do you mean?" I ask.

He raises his eyes and meets mine. Passion burns in them, white-hot desire, but more than that I see pain.

"Now that you've... the Dragons," he says, skipping over saying the uncomfortable parts.

"Oh, my God!" I exclaim, slapping his arm.

"What?" he asks, confusion replacing the desire.

"Are you serious?" I ask. "Even if I did, why does that have to affect us?"

"It's... I..." he shakes his head. "Look, it's fine. You're a grown woman, I don't own you, and I have no claim on you. You have to make your decisions, and I have to respect that."

"What if I don't want to decide?" I ask.

"Aviella, you have to, eventually," he says, shaking his head.

"Do I?" I counter.

Efram stops, frowning, then he looks away.

"This won't be for long, I'll catch up to you once I'm finished," he says, pointedly changing the subject.

I don't push. This is exactly why I can't choose. If I pick one, then things will fall apart with the others. I want them all. I don't want things to change between us. How could I pick one when they're all so special, when each one is unique? Each of them has a place in my heart. Shaking my head, I stand up and grab the bag, shoving the last items in, then slinging it over my shoulder.

"I should go," I say.

"Yeah," he agrees, rising to his feet.

We're inches apart. His presence is close, but comfortable. My feelings for him are like a sore tooth, throbbing and raw, but I can't leave it alone. He looks down into my eyes, and an urge grips me. Screw it.

Rising on my toes, I plant my lips on his. He stiffens, lips forming a hard line, but I ignore his reaction and shove my tongue into his mouth. His arms enclose me, his mouth responding to mine. His cock stiffens and digs into my abdomen. That's more like it. Our kiss continues as his hands roam down my back and cup my ass. Hooking my arms around his neck, I hold him close and tight. If we're going to be apart, I want him to have something solid to remember me by.

My body wants more, so much more, I've been dancing this edge forever and still haven't given over to it, but now isn't the time either. At last our need for air forces us apart. His eyes burn like twin coals, hot with desire and need. He swallows hard, and one hand goes to his lips with a gentle touch. He steps back, but I see a shiver before he does.

"You won't forget me?" I ask, softly.

"Never," he says, his voice deep and husky.

"Good," I say, a tear slipping down my cheek. "I can't do this without you. Whatever in the hell this is."

He wipes the tear with his thumb, then his hand is cupping my cheek. My heart breaks inside as fear grips me. Fear I won't see him again, fear I won't see any of them again. That I'll make the wrong move, or say the wrong thing, or lose control of my powers at the wrong moment. That I'll screw it all up, somehow, because that's what I'm infinitely good at doing.

"I'm yours," he whispers. "Always."

Unable to speak, I nod and place my hand over his on my cheek, nuzzling into him. When at last we part, we share one last, much more chaste, kiss. I watch him walking away until

I can't see him anymore, then I follow the directions I was given to meet Silas and the Dragons.

∾

"The texts are ancient," Shen says. "Even by your standards."

He eyes Silas, who smiles and shrugs.

"Good God! I get it, they're really old. You've been saying that and little else for an hour now. Do they *tell* us anything new?" I cry out in exasperation.

"Yes," Alaric says.

I glare at him, waiting for him to say something, anything.

"This situation is new," Tynan says. "Aviella, you have to understand, we're in unknown ground here."

"I've spent my entire life in unknown ground!" I shout. "Does it matter? No. It's called life, you never know what's going to happen next."

"That is not our way," Shen says.

"Who cares!" I throw my hands up whirling on him. "What's the information? What do we know now? Can we get to the point, please?"

"Aviella, calm and control are called for," Silas says.

"You shut up," I say, wagging a finger at him. "You're an observer in this. They're pissing me off, and I don't have time to sit around waiting while they drag their feet. Either they know something, or they don't. If not, fine, but let's move on to the next thing!"

"Aviella—" Alaric says.

"Nope, not going to hear it," I say, holding my hand up palm facing him. "My Dad is out there, and he's hurt. You all saw it, so did I. You all said you'd help, now out with it."

"You're tied to a blood-line that is… ancient," Tynan says.

He stops looking at the others.

"Yeah?" I prompt. He shakes his head, clears his throat, then gestures futilely. "Well?"

"Our fates are tied to you," Shen picks up.

"Destiny, yours, ours, they're intertwined in ways we never expected," Alaric continues.

"The symbols told you all that?" I ask.

"Yes," Tynan says, picking up the conversation again.

"Okay great, what about my Dad? Any luck locating him?" I ask.

"You don't understand," Alaric says.

"What we're trying to tell you," Shen continues.

"We have uncovered your fate, why you're here," Tynan says.

"And how it affects us," Alaric says.

"Okay, I really hate it when you guys talk like you have one brain or something. Can you just... not?" I ask, feeling out of sorts with it. They're like some kind of horrid triplets, though they look nothing alike.

They look at each other, then shrug, again as one.

"Okay," Tynan agrees.

I stare at each of them, waiting for one of them to pick the conversation back up, but no one says a word.

"Oh seriously? Come on!" I exclaim.

"You're here to save the world, Aviella," Tynan says. "Figuratively and literally."

My stomach drops to the floor, and a hysterical urge to laugh comes over me. A titter slips out. Yeah, a freaking titter. I'm not holding that against myself because a bomb has been dropped on me.

"Right," I laugh. "Save the world. Me. The outcast. The orphan."

The laughter becomes higher pitched and takes on a more maniacal aspect. The Dragons look at each other, unsure what to make of my hysterics. That's okay, I don't know either. It's insane, but then inside something resonates, and it feels right. Which must mean that I'm nuts, totally off the deep end. Right? What sane person thinks the fate of the world rests on their shoulders? How about, not a damn one. Right, so either I'm insane or he is. I'm voting on him. What do you do with an insane Dragon Horseman of the Apocalypse?

"Aviella," Silas says, placing a hand on my arm.

Warmth flows into me from that point of contact, and I latch onto it like a sailor clinging to the rail in a tempest.

"It's a joke, right?" I ask, the urge to throw myself into the yawning black pit inside my mind and blow this Popsicle stand is almost more than I can resist.

"It's not a joke," Shen says.

"Our fate is tied to you," Tynan says. "We will help you. We must."

Pulling myself mentally off the edge of the black void I'm looking into, I take a deep breath and let it out slowly.

"I have to save my Dad," I say. "Everything else can go hang. He's my priority."

"We expected as much," Tynan says. "We will help you but for his safety, we must first assure yours."

"From what? What is it that's after me? Where is my Dad? What do we do now?" The questions, the ones I've been holding back, pour out of me in a flood.

"Darkness," Shen says. "Dark forces that like the status quo—they're winning. Claiming souls and sowing chaos."

"Isn't that what you guys do, pretty much by definition?" I ask.

"No, nowhere near it," Tynan answers.

They don't seem offended by my jab, which is probably good. Pissing off the Horsemen could be a monumentally stupid mistake right now. I'm not sure I care—I'm so sick of being 'special.' I want my Dad. I have to save him.

"Trust us," Shen says.

"We're working as fast as we can to uncover as much information as we can about your role in the end times. As fast as we can."

"Great," I say, shaking my head. "Perfect, lovely! What about my Dad?"

They look at each other, but no one has an answer. Fine. If it's on me then it's on me. I'll figure out my own plan, and they can do their best to keep up. I don't know who or what has him, but they better get ready. I'm coming, and I'm bringing hell with me.

∼

Continue *the Power of Twelve* series in book three,
Apocalypse the Believer

∼

ABOUT THE AUTHOR

USA Today Bestselling Author of fantasy and scifi romance, Miranda Martin's books feature larger than life heroes with out-of-this-world anatomy and smart heroines destined to save the world. As a little girl she would sneak off with her nose in a book, dreaming of magical realms. Today she brings those fantasies to life and adores every fan who chooses to live in them for a while.

She was born and raised in southern Virginia, but as a veteran she's traveled to places like Korea, Hawaii and good 'ole Texas. Now she's settled in Kansas, the heart of America, with her husband and daughters. Her favorite animals are dragons, unicorns, and cats. If she's not writing, you can still find her tucked away somewhere with a warm blanket and her nose in a book.

Get in touch!
mirandamartinromance.com
miranda@mirandamartinromance.com

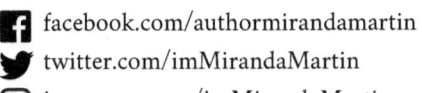

facebook.com/authormirandamartin
twitter.com/imMirandaMartin
instagram.com/imMirandaMartin

ALSO BY MIRANDA MARTIN

USA TODAY BESTSELLING AUTHOR

Red Planet Dragon's of Tajss Series
Red Planet Jungle Series
The Power of Twelve Series
The Alva Series
Dragon's & Phoenixes Series